THE
WHITES
OF
THEIR
EYES

BENJAMIN PRATT & THE
KEEPERS OF THE SCHOOL

THE WHITES OF THEIR EYES

BOOK 3

ANDREW CLEMENTS

ILLUSTRATED BY ADAM STOWER

Atheneum Books for Young Readers
New York London Toronto Sydney New Delhi

ATHENEUM BOOKS FOR YOUNG READERS
An imprint of Simon & Schuster Children's Publishing Division
1230 Avenue of the Americas, New York, New York 10020
For information about special discounts for bulk purchases, please contact Simon & Schuster Special Sales at 1-866-506-1949 or business@simonandschuster.com.
The Simon & Schuster Speakers Bureau can bring authors to your live event. For more information or to book an event, contact the Simon & Schuster Speakers Bureau at 1-866-248-3049 or visit our website at www.simonspeakers.com.
Book design by Sonia Chaghatzbanian
The text for this book is set in Garamond.
The illustrations for this book are rendered in pen and ink.
Manufactured in the United States of America
1211 FFG
First Edition
10 9 8 7 6 5 4 3 2 1
CIP data for this book is available from the Library of Congress.
ISBN 978-1-4169-3888-0

For Karl and Donna Hellman
—A. C.

THE
WHITES
OF
THEIR
EYES

CHAPTER 1

Direct Orders

I must be crazy!

Benjamin Pratt had gotten the idea two hours earlier while he was sitting on the couch. He and his mom had been watching *The Sea Hawk*, a big, old-fashioned swashbuckler. The hero of the movie, Captain Thorpe, was unstoppable. Huge sailing ships blasted cannons at each other, pirates with pistols and cutlasses fought to the death, and Captain Thorpe was always right there in the thick of the action. Even at his most desperate moments, the man never lost hope. He risked everything again and again.

Yeah, Ben thought, but that was in a movie.

Because here he was in real life, risking everything at eleven forty-five on a Friday night. He was standing outside a door near the northeast corner of the Captain Duncan Oakes School, dressed in black from head to toe like some sixth-grade ninja assassin. His mom thought he was sound asleep in his bed. He wasn't. He was about to commit a crime, about to become guilty of breaking and entering.

Well, not actually *breaking* and entering. He had a key . . . if he could only find the right one. He didn't dare use his flashlight, and the energy-saving bulb in the grimy lantern beside the door threw more shadows than light—which was probably good, considering what he was up to. The key ring jangled as he tried key after key, and he was glad for the sound of waves, murmuring against the seawall seventy feet away. He tapped his tongue against the back of his front teeth—a nervous habit.

Jill was going to be mad. Nine days ago Ben's whole life had been turned upside down, and Jill was the one friend he had turned to for help. She wasn't going to be mad because he was sneaking into the school, but because he was doing it without her. Well . . . too bad. Had *she* invited him the other night, when she had pulled up all those surveying stakes from the grounds on the south side of the school? No.

Of course, if she *had* invited him, he probably would have tried to talk her out of it. And Jill might have tried to talk him out of going into the school too. But ever since Mrs. Keane had given him her husband's keys, Ben had been dying to use them.

Dying to use them—that thought brought half a smile to his lips, but only for a second. It was a gruesome joke. Mr. Keane, the school janitor, had actually died just eight days ago. Hours before his death, he had made Ben swear to do all he could to save the Oakes School. Mr. Keane had given Ben a gold coin inscribed with these words: IF ATTACKED, LOOK NOR'-NOR'EAST FROM AMIDSHIPS ON THE UPPER DECK. The flip side of the coin read, FIRST AND ALWAYS, MY SCHOOL BELONGS TO THE CHILDREN. DEFEND IT. DUNCAN OAKES, 1783.

That command came from Captain Oakes himself. . . . So really, Ben thought, I'm not a burglar tonight. I'm one of the Keepers of the School, and I'm obeying a direct order from the founder.

The school needed defending. This building

had stood next to Barclay Bay since before the Revolutionary War, and Captain Oakes had turned it into a school in 1783. In less than three weeks a wrecking ball was going to smash the place to bits—a huge part of Edgeport's history, destroyed in one day. And why? To construct a big, noisy theme park on the school's oceanfront land.

Ben gritted his teeth at that thought. It made what he was doing tonight feel like less of a crime. Because it wasn't like he was going inside to vandalize or steal. He was only going in to look, to search. There were secrets all over this building, things that had been lying hidden since the 1780s, things that just might be able to keep the school from being torn down—and keep the harbor from turning into a tourist trap.

"Stop that!"

Ben froze, then looked right.

A woman. Over on the sidewalk next to the seawall in front of the school. She was yelling at a little gray poodle—it was off its leash, running around in circles. The lady hadn't seen him . . . but the dog might be dangerous.

Ben slowly moved right, away from the door and the dim light. He eased onto his knees, then stretched out flat in the shadows close to the wall. The doorstep was a wide granite block, but it was only about six inches high. Still, any cover was better than none. His heart was thumping, but he lay perfectly still, eyes pressed shut, trying not to breathe.

"Arf! . . . rrrrr . . . rrrrrArf!"

Ben had a dog, a little corgi named Nelson. He knew dog sounds, and *that* was the sound of worry—or anger. He opened one eye.

The tiny dog was streaking across the lawn, straight at him.

"ArrArrArr! ArrArrArrArr! ArrArrArrArrArr!"

It stopped inches from his face, lips curled, shoulders hunched, ready to pounce.

"ArrArrArr! ArrArrArrArr!"

Ben smelled the Kibbles on its breath. He imagined himself with itty-bitty bite marks all over his face, being shoved into the back of a police car.

"Noodles! *Bad boy!* You get back over here!"

The lady clapped her hands twice, and with one more angry "Arf," Noodles trotted away, the proud watchdog.

The woman clipped his leash on and they left, walking south.

I should go home—that was Ben's first thought once the coast was clear. He lay there, still trembling.

But really, what better time to search the school than right now? He'd brought extra flashlight batteries. He could explore for hours with no interruptions—no teachers, no schedules, and no Lyman.

Mr. Lyman.

This was the beginning of the Memorial Day weekend, so even if he didn't get inside the school tonight, Ben was guaranteed three whole days of not having to deal with Lyman—which was a huge relief. Ever since Mr. Keane's death, the new assistant janitor had been tracking him and Jill, trying to follow their every move. The guy was like a bad smell, the kind that gets stuck in your nose and stays there for days, weeks.

The thought of Lyman got Ben got to his feet. He scanned the harbor side for other late-night visitors. All clear.

Edging back into the light, he quickly tried another key in the lock . . . nope. And then another . . . not that one.

Their conflict with Lyman was out in the open now. He was posing as the school janitor, but he was actually working for Glennley Entertainment Group, the company behind the amusement park scheme.

Ben tried another key . . . nope.

Months ago Lyman had heard Mr. Keane muttering about some sort of secret plan, a way to stop the demolition; and Lyman knew that Ben had been the last person at school who talked with Mr. Keane the day he died. And then Lyman had seen Ben and Jill snooping around the school.

There had been a showdown in the library before school today—was that just *this* morning?

Ben shook his head. Friday morning seemed like a hundred years ago. After this morning's

confrontation, Lyman understood that Ben and
Jill were onto him, that he was spying for the
Glennley Group.

It was a private little war inside the Oakes
School—Ben and Jill against Mr. Lyman. So far,
Lyman had no idea what they were looking for,
or if they had actually found anything. But he
had strong suspicions, and that was making the
man . . . upset.

Maybe *this* key . . . no, not even close.

Ben smiled grimly. He and Jill *had* found
things. By decoding the directions on Mr. Keane's
coin they'd found a large iron key, and most
important, a list of clues—clues about objects that
had been hidden around the school, "safeguards"
for defending it.

Solving the first clue had been tough, but
they'd located the first safeguard. It was a secret
codicil, a document from 1783 that changed the
captain's original will. So they'd made some actual
progress . . . but Lyman was making it more and
more difficult to search—and secrecy was critical.

Arrgh! So many keys, and that stupid dog had
made him lose his place on the key ring.

Three more—that was the deal Ben made with

himself. It was almost midnight now. Three more keys, and if none of them worked, he'd go home. Because he could always sneak over here again tomorrow night, right?

The first key didn't fit into the lock.

The second key . . . *yes*, a perfect fit! But it wouldn't turn.

And the third key . . . didn't fit.

So that was that.

Ben turned away with a shrug and started for home. He'd made an honest effort, a brave attempt. He'd really tried. He had.

As he walked across the school grounds and into the deep shadows of the trees, Ben thought again about Captain Thorpe, *The Sea Hawk*. And then he remembered Captain Oakes, the founder of the school.

Ben stopped and turned around. He had sworn to do everything he could to save this school. He scanned the area, then hurried back to the doorstep.

He tried another key. And another. And another. And another. None of them even fit into the keyhole.

Still, he kept at it, and after sixteen more tries,

a key slipped smoothly into the lock. He twisted . . . and it turned. Ben pulled the door open.

He looked over his shoulder, took one last breath of cool night air, then stepped inside. The latch clicked behind him.

CHAPTER 2

Schooled

Ben stopped just inside the door. In the dim light he took careful note of the key he'd just used—important information.

He still had one hand on the crash bar. It wasn't warm in the school, but he was sweating and his mouth was dry. If he pushed the bar and backed up three feet, he'd be outside again. He could be home and in his bed in ten minutes.

No.

He'd sneaked out tonight so he could have the whole school to himself, so he could explore for as long as he wanted to. And here he was.

But . . . maybe I should have brought rubber gloves.

Dumb thought. His fingerprints were already all over the school, along with Jill's and hundreds of other kids'.

An alarm system . . . maybe the police are on their way right now.

But he hadn't seen any cameras or sensors around the school, and he had looked very carefully. Ever since he and Jill discovered that Lyman had made a secret visit to his dad's sailboat, they had both been on the lookout for microphones, webcams—any suspicious-looking electronics.

He was out of excuses. It wasn't even that dark inside the school—almost brighter than outside. Every door and hallway entrance had a glowing red exit sign.

Ben knew the clue for each safeguard practically by heart, but he pulled a folded index card from his pocket anyway. He clicked on his flash-

After five bells sound, time to sit down.
After four times four, tread up one more.
After three hooks pass, one will be brass.
After two tides spin, a man walks in.
After one still star, horizons afar.

light, covering most of the beam with his thumb. As he read, he noticed his hands were shaking.

They'd solved the "five bells" clue a couple of days ago, and they'd found the addition to Captain Oakes's will. That little sheet of vellum might have some real power, but using it would definitely complicate things. It would mean taking the whole war public, and *that* would mean the Glennley Group would fight with lawyers and money and politics—instead of just relying on Lyman.

So the plan was to keep on hunting—that's what he and Jill had decided. And the directions about searching for the safeguards were clear: Look for each one in order. So . . .

After four times four, tread up one more.

They'd talked about this next clue. "After four times four"—that was sixteen; then "one more" totaled seventeen—ridiculously simple math.

And the "tread up" part? Also simple . . . possibly. Because that word "tread"? Yes, it could just mean "to walk." But it could also mean the tread of a staircase, the flat part you stepped on. Which was why Ben turned right at the main corridor by the library and walked toward the north stair-well. There weren't that many places in the school where you could walk up seventeen treads—if that was what the clue even meant. But he had to start the search somewhere.

Listening to the creaking floor and his echoing footsteps, it felt strange to be alone in the empty school so late at night.

But he wasn't frightened, not really. Sure, his heart was beating faster than usual, but he was fine . . . just fine. Being alone in the dark had never bothered him much. Unless he started remembering scary movies.

Ben shoved that thought out of his head as he opened the heavy fire door at the bottom of the north stairwell. Six feet straight ahead of him a flight of stairs rose to a landing. Using his flashlight beam as a pointer, he counted the steps . . . ten.

He trotted up to the landing, turned left and left again, then counted the next flight that went to the second floor . . . another ten. Twenty steps, twenty treads.

He walked up six steps from the landing, then went one more and stood on step number seven-teen—"After four times four, tread up one more."

Bouncing on that seventeenth tread with all his weight, he listened—any squeaks or rattles or clanks? Nothing suspicious at all.

He knelt down on step number fifteen, then leaned forward. Using his light, he examined the seventeenth tread, his nose inches from the surface.

It was a solid rectangle of wood, some kind of oak—Ben knew that much. And it was super tough, because after more than two hundred years of heavy foot traffic, it was barely worn—none of the treads were. He checked the rounded edges, tapped on the vertical board rising behind the step, inspected every nail head, every knot and ripple in the texture of the wood.

There was nothing unusual. And tread number seventeen was identical to eighteen, sixteen, and fifteen—they were all the same.

But of course, this was just one staircase. Maybe the clue was linked to the south stairwell. Or . . . maybe he should start from the second floor and work up to the third. Or . . . maybe start at the third floor and count *down* sixteen steps, then go back *up* a step—except . . . that wouldn't be going "up one more" . . . would it?

Hmm.

Tons of possibilities, but he had lots of time. So it probably made the most sense to just . . .

The cell phone in his front pocket made a quick double vibration—a new text. Ben got it out, and then stared at the bluish screen:

My mommy?!

The name and number of the sender was blocked. The phone vibrated again, then again, and again.

Not a text, a regular phone call. And this time the caller ID was crystal clear: EDGEPORT POLICE DEPT.

Ben panicked.

Blasting down the stairs three at a time, he slammed through the fire door, then skidded right and ran. At the causeway into the Annex, he went right again and streaked for the first exit. Bursting outside, he almost ran into Captain Oakes's large granite tombstone, which was right in the middle of the playground. He adjusted his course and made a beeline for home, running down the middle of the lighted pathway, but ready to take off into the trees if he had to.

He still gripped the phone in his hand—12:05 now.

There was no traffic as he shot across School Street, but a car was coming at him along Walnut Street, still half a block away. He hated to waste even a moment, but what if it was a police car? He ducked into some bushes.

The car sailed past, just a white sedan. Running again, he felt Mr. Keane's heavy key ring bouncing in the front pocket of his black hoodie. At Central Street he had to hide in the shadow of a big SUV for almost a minute, waiting for some traffic to clear.

Two houses from home, he slowed to a walk. If he didn't approach softly, Nelson would get spooked and bark his head off.

Just outside the kitchen door, he made a little kissing sound and whispered, "Good boy, Nelson, it's me."

He heard a soft whine of recognition through the door, then opened it slowly and moved inside. "Stay, Nelson, stay."

Ben shed his shoes and clothes, then pulled on the pajamas he'd left in a canvas shopping bag hanging from a hook. Sweaty and shivering, he stuffed the whole ninja outfit back into the bag.

Now for the hardest part—the barefoot trip up to his attic room. This house had been built in the 1820s. Even though it was newer than the school by almost eighty years, it hadn't been constructed as well, and the floors were a lot creakier.

Staying close to the wall in the hallway from the kitchen, Ben stopped at the closet. He pulled the door open slowly and stuffed the bag with his clothes and the keys back behind the coats. He closed the door, then remembered—his cell phone! He opened the closet and rummaged in the bag till he found it.

Ben had made a careful study of the front stairs over the years—mostly around Christmas. The bottom step had a terrible groaning creak, so he stretched completely over it. The next three steps just chirped a little as long as he stayed close to the wall on the right. The fifth step was another groaner, and the sixth was even worse. He had to stretch over the fifth, and get to the far left on the sixth and put as much weight as possible onto the handrail . . . *rwaarrk* . . . it always did that, no matter what.

He stopped and held his breath—no sound from his mom's room.

He took the next three steps close to the left wall, then stretched over the very top step, and he was in the upstairs hall. He turned left, tiptoeing and staying close to the wall.

He was beginning to breathe easier. He glanced at his cell phone—12:09.

Brrnnnngg!

The sound of the house telephone bit him like a wasp. He leaped the last four feet to the attic doorway, sprinted up the narrow stairs, and dove under his covers.

Heart fluttering, he strained to listen—his mom's voice, then the heavy plastic handset dropping back onto its cradle.

Her bedroom door creaked opened, and when the hall light clicked on, a glow filtered up into his room.

"Ben? . . . Ben?"

"Yeah? Wh-what?" He didn't have to do much acting to sound tired and worried.

"Oh, it's nothing, sweetie. Just wanted to check on you. Go on back to sleep."

"Okay. Love you, Mom."

"I love you, too. G'night."

Lying there in his soft bed, his heartbeats slowed. Once his breathing calmed down, he could hear the sea breeze rustling the new maple leaves outside his window. The house was quiet again, and he felt safe. But he had to face some unpleasant questions.

That text? It must have come from Lyman—who else?

But how had he gotten the police to call him—or had he faked that somehow?

He definitely had the number to Ben's cell phone, which he could have easily copied off the emergency contact card in the nurse's office at school. . . .

But how had the guy known he was *there*, at the school?

Had he been outside in the dark on the school grounds somewhere, like a cop on a stakeout? Seemed unlikely . . .

But wherever the man was, *somehow* he had known Ben was inside the school.

There *was* one logical answer: Before leaving for the long weekend, Lyman could have rigged up his own private security system—like door alarms . . . maybe he'd set up cameras, too. Which would mean Lyman might have a picture of him sneaking in, maybe even a movie. . . .

And that bit about calling his "mommy," using his own mother against him like a weapon? That was really low . . . but very effective.

Jill.

Ben groaned silently. Maybe he didn't really need to mention any of this. . . . No, he'd have to tell her. But she was really going to yell about it.

From the start, Jill had said they should never underestimate Lyman. He was a trained professional, a serious corporate spy with a big budget and access to all kinds of gadgets and equipment.

Well, he thought, *we've* got a budget too.

It was true. Ben had met Tom Benton at Mr. Keane's funeral. He'd been the janitor at Oakes School before Mr. Keane. Tom was retired, and Ben had helped him to recover a rusty tackle box loaded with rare old coins—enough to buy all the antispying equipment they would ever need. Tom was now the official treasurer for the Keepers of the School.

He smiled as he remembered what Jill had said when he'd called and told her about the coins: "Great—maybe *we* can hire a spy to spy on Lyman!"

Clearly, the Keepers needed *something* to help level the battlefield.

A level battlefield.

Ben liked that thought. It was an idea he could get to sleep on.

He stretched and yawned.

Yes, Mr. Lyman, you are clever and experienced, and you won tonight's battle. But this new phase of our little war? It's only just beginning.

CHAPTER 3

Day Off

Ben stood with his mouth open, staring. He looked quickly from his dad's face to his mom's, then back to the beach just north of the marina.

"Really?" he gasped. "I mean, *really*?"

His mom and dad each nodded again, both of them beaming.

Ben sped off across the wooden planks of the pier. At the very edge he stopped and ran back and hugged his mom, then his dad.

"Thanks! This is just . . . just *incredible*!"

He took off again, this time leaping from the pier down onto the beach. He sprinted the last twenty yards, and there, sitting on its two-wheeled

dolly just above the high-water mark, was a sailboat, *his* sailboat.

He did a quick scan of the hull. Not new, but it was in great shape—fiberglass, with no dings, no patches, no cracks. The tiller and centerboard were made of black epoxy—nice equipment, clean and sharp. He dropped onto the sand beside the dinghy and looked up at the underside—the white gel coat was bright and smooth. And back topside again, the long blue canvas gear bag was very clean . . . *too* clean.

His folks had walked over, and he looked up and pointed at the gear bag. "Is that . . ."

"Yup," said his dad. "Brand-new. I located the hull and the dolly, and your mom picked out the mast and boom and sprit—plus a racing sail. First-class gear for a first-class sailor."

Ben had to gulp back his emotions. The boat was amazing—his own Optimist! But that wasn't what brought a lump to his throat. It was because his parents had teamed up to get it. They'd been separated for more than two months now, but they'd done *this* together. For him.

"Really, this is too much!"

His dad shook his head. "It's way overdue."

"Absolutely!" his mom said. "Think of it as a combined birthday and Christmas present for a wonderful son."

"And maybe *next* year's birthday and Christmas too," his dad added.

"So, can I take her out?" Ben asked. "Like, today?"

"Sure," said his dad, "but you've got a couple chores to do first."

Ben hugged his mom. "Thanks again, Mom. This is great, the best ever."

"You're welcome, sweetheart. I've got to go now, but I'll be in touch during the week, all right? If you want to stop over some day after school, just let me know."

He nodded. "I will."

But Ben didn't actually know if he was allowed to do that, stop over after school. His parents had worked out a deal about where he lived, and he shifted places every other week. This was his week to live with Dad at the marina on the family's sailboat . . . or was it just *Dad's* sailboat now?

She smiled at Ben, nodded awkwardly at his dad, then turned and walked across the sand toward the wooden steps by the parking lot.

She'd drive home to their house now . . . or was it just *her* house now?

Every Saturday he had to say good-bye to his mom or his dad. It always hurt, and nothing could make it stop. Not even a new sailboat.

Ben looked at his dad. "So, it's okay to just leave the boat here awhile?"

"I told Kevin I was sure you'd want to take it out this afternoon. He's keeping an eye on it, and I got you a space in the storage shed over there. It's fifteen dollars a month, which is a really good deal. I'll pay the rent for June, but then it'll be up to you, okay?"

"Sure, that's great, Dad. Thanks."

The sailboat had been a complete surprise . . . although it *had* seemed sort of odd when his mom got out of the car and walked onto the pier with him. She usually just dropped him at the gate near the marina's security shed.

"Come on, let's get your stuff out to the boat." His dad vaulted up onto the pier, then reached down and gave Ben a hand up. "There's not much in the way of chores today, just polishing some brightwork on deck. Did you have lunch before you left home?"

Ben heard the tiny pause before his dad said the word "home."

"Yup."

"Then you could be out on the water pretty quick, if you look alive. I'll get your bags."

"It's okay, I'll get 'em," Ben said.

"Good. See you onboard."

Ben walked to where he'd dropped his things. He pulled on his backpack and then hoisted his green canvas duffel bag. It was loaded with a week's worth of clean clothes, and after ten steps he wished he'd let his dad help. But he'd tossed Mr. Keane's keys into the top of the bag at the last second, and if his dad spotted them or even heard them jangling around, it might lead to difficult questions.

Walking out onto the floating pier, he replayed last night's adventure at the school. If he'd gotten caught, there certainly would *not* have been a happy here's-your-new-boat scene on the beach today . . . still, he wished he'd had time to look in the south stairwell . . . and weren't there some other stairways too? He tried to remember the drawings in that book at the school library, the one about the construction of the school . . . no, couldn't recall.

As he turned onto the narrow catwalk alongside the *Tempus Fugit*, he pushed all that out of his mind. Today he was *not* going to be Benjamin Pratt, Keeper of the School. It was Memorial Day weekend, and the sun was shining.

Today he was just a very happy kid whose mom and dad had teamed up and given him his very own sailboat.

He deserved a day off, and the ocean was waiting.

CHAPTER 4

Rough Water

It was nearly eighty degrees, only a few high clouds, and a steady ten-knot breeze from the southwest—perfect conditions to take his Optimist out for the first time. Ben waved to his dad, who was watching from the deck of the *Tempus Fugit* halfway out on the pier.

He waded out about thirty feet, keeping both hands on the gunwale while he watched the sail and the waves. He was waiting for the right moment to shove off and hop aboard. The water was cold, but he hardly noticed.

"Hey, Ben! Ahoy there!"

Rats!

It was Jill. They had planned to meet here at

his dad's on Saturday afternoon, and he'd completely forgotten.

"Hey, hi, Jill."

Ben pulled the bow of the boat around into the wind and let the sail flap.

He thought he'd hidden his disappointment, but Jill got the whole picture in half a second. As he began walking the boat back toward the beach, she held up her hand.

"It's okay. I tried calling first, but your phone was off."

"Oh, right—sorry."

He'd left his phone off on purpose so he wouldn't have to tell her about last night. Also, he didn't like the feeling that Lyman could call or text anytime he wanted.

"Listen," she said. "I'll come back later, maybe around three?"

That sounded great—she lived only a few blocks away. But as she turned and started walking across the beach, Ben had another thought.

"Hey," he called, "you should come out with me. This is my new boat—my folks just got it for me. Really, come out sailing."

"Now?" She made a face. "No, I'm—I don't have the right clothes or anything. Some other time, okay?"

"Look, just run out to the boat and ask my dad for some gear. There's tons of stuff that'll fit you. It'll only take a couple minutes."

Jill began backing away. "But the boat's so . . . small. It's made for one person, right?"

"Yeah, when you're racing. But if it's just for fun, two kids'll fit fine. C'mon, it's a perfect day. You'll like it."

"I really don't think . . ."

"Unless it's too scary for you . . . 'cause I

don't want you to feel worried or anything." Ben grinned and shrugged.

Jill glared at him.

"Wait there."

She stalked over to the pier, climbed up, and then trotted out to the sailboat. Ben saw her talk to his dad, then he went below and she followed.

The *Tempus Fugit* was a thirty-four-foot yawl that his dad had bought before he got married. These days it took a lot of work to keep the boat seaworthy.

Still, the family had taken it on some pretty long voyages the past few summers—all the way to Nova Scotia one year. Back when there *was* a family . . .

Ben hated that last thought, but he couldn't help it. Stuff like that kept popping into his head.

He held the bow of the Optimist and looked north along the shore. His eye stopped on Oakes School, the largest building on Edgeport's waterfront. All he wanted to do was take his new boat for a simple little spin around the bay and stop thinking about that place for an hour or so. But Jill showing up brought everything rushing back, all the problems they'd been dealing with over the past nine days.

Tall Ships Ahoy!—that would be the name of the new theme park. If the school was torn down.

Ben understood much better now how the situation had gotten to this point, and how the Glennley Group's lawyers had weaseled their way past Captain Oakes's will. It was really very simple—one word: money. They had spent over thirty-five million dollars up front, and then promised millions and millions more in the future—tons of local jobs, increased tourism, more tax income—*lots* of money.

Not that he had anything against money . . . without money, would he have his new sailboat? No, it wasn't the money itself. It was how the money was used. Because something good and useful was going to be destroyed here. Real history was being swept away, replaced by fake history—plus noise, plus pollution, plus loads of other changes.

Ben also felt like he was starting to understand Captain Oakes. With all the care he'd put into the place, he must have felt that the school was the most important accomplishment of his whole life. Ben could see why the man had wanted to make sure the school stayed put, way off into the future. It was something he intended to give to everyone in the whole town. Yes, first it was a school, but it was also just a beautiful, unspoiled stretch of shoreline. People came and fished, even had weekend picnics on the school grounds. It was free for everyone.

The Glennley Group was going to put up fences. They were going to push a big concrete pier out into the harbor, then load it up with a giant Ferris wheel and all sorts of other rides and attractions.

Ben shook his head. It was hard not to feel discouraged. They were up against huge odds.

And Lyman? He was their biggest problem, especially now. Because he knew that they were hunting for things at the school—and *he* knew that *they* knew that *he* knew.

If only there was some way to . . .

"So where do I sit in this tub?"

Ben snapped his eyes back to the beach, and there was Jill, hands on her hips. She was wearing a set of his old waterproofs, a faded Red Sox cap, and a bright orange life vest.

"Calling my boat a tub is a great way to get dunked," Ben said with a smile, only half kidding.

"First we have to take the boat out where it's deep enough to start off."

"You mean, *walk*?"

"Unless you can fly."

"But . . . my feet'll get wet."

"Sailing a small boat and being wet are pretty much the same thing," said Ben. "You get used to it."

"Sounds great."

It was low tide, so even after pushing the boat about forty feet from shore, the water was only two feet deep. The breeze was running mostly northward along the beach, so there wasn't much surf to deal with. Ben fastened the rudder in place.

"Okay, now!" They both hopped in, and he pushed the centerboard down into its slot. He pointed and said, "Sit down there on the floor, and watch your head." He tapped the aluminum pole along the bottom of the sail. "This is the boom, and it swings from side to side a lot. I'll give you a warning when it's coming overhead, but keep a sharp eye on it."

"Aye, aye, cap'n," Jill said.

She was mocking him, but Ben didn't care. He'd never been called captain before. And it was true. Here he was, at the helm of his very own boat—Captain Benjamin Pratt!

He gave the tiller a few quick shoves to angle the hull more across the wind. He paid out the sheet a little, and the breeze puffed the sail tight and smooth. The dinghy leaped forward across the waves, and in no time they were a hundred yards out into Barclay Bay.

"Wow!" Jill said. "This thing really flies!"

She wasn't mocking now. With salt water rushing past and the air tossing sharp spray into her face, the raw power of the wind and the waves impressed her—the ocean did that to everybody. In his few years as a solo sailor, Ben had learned to be humble out on the water. And never to get comfortable. So many things could go wrong— like what had happened to Robert Gerritt during last weekend's sailing race.

Sure, the guy had been taking risks, pushing his boat way too hard in rough conditions. Still, you don't expect to drown during a junior Opti- mist race. And if it hadn't been for Ben, Robert would have.

But he couldn't think about that now. He had a boat to steer. Down to the south there was a regatta—big fixed-keel yachts. It was a broad course, plus there was a lot of spectator traffic.

Best to stay well away from the action.

"Want to sail up past the school?"

"Sure," said Jill. "This is really amazing, to go this fast with just the wind? *Very* cool!"

Ben wanted to tell her about *real* sailing—this was barely moving. Because an Optimist could handle some pretty wild air. He wanted to explain why they should be constantly shifting their weight around to keep the boat planing on its best surfaces, and then show her the difference between a beam reach and a broad reach, and maybe how to steer close to the wind.

He kept his mouth shut. For now, he'd let her enjoy the ride. If she liked it, there'd be time for sailing school another day. Still, she had to know a few things for safety.

"Okay, I'm going to come about in a

few seconds, which means I'm going to turn the boat so the wind'll be pushing on the other side of the sail. That lets us sail in a different direction, which is called tacking. And this boom's gonna swing across the hull. So when I yell, 'Ready about,' you switch to this side of the boat, and I'll move to that side. And be ready to duck, okay?"

She nodded, and Ben barked, "Ready about!"

He jammed the tiller to starboard, which swung the bow to port as the boom flew across the hull. Jill ducked and scrambled to the other side, and Ben sat up on the opposite gunwale, tucking his feet under the toe straps.

Now the bow was aimed straight toward the school.

"The town's beautiful," Jill said. "I've never seen it from out here."

"Really?" Ben said. "You haven't been on the bay before? Ever?"

"Nope. We go north for vacations. My family has a cabin on Lake Winnipesaukee. We water-ski and canoe and stuff, but we don't have a sailboat. It's a big lake, but nothing like this."

Ben couldn't imagine living beside the ocean and not getting out onto it. If his parents hadn't had the *Tempus Fugit*, he'd have found something—a rowboat, a kayak, even a blow-up raft with a paddle—anything to get onto the water.

As they came in toward land, Jill said, "If you'd had your phone on, I could have told you some good news this morning."

"Oh yeah? What?"

"We can get into the school this afternoon at three thirty. The Historical Society is moving a bunch of old tools out of there today. My mom's on the committee, so I asked if we could come along and help carry stuff. And get this—Lyman won't be there. Pretty great, huh?"

"Wow, yeah," said Ben, "sounds terrific." He paused a beat. "But I should tell you something."

He hesitated, and Jill could tell he didn't want to go on.

"Yes . . . ," she said, "keep talking."

"Well, I sneaked into the school last night, and around midnight—"

"You *what?*"

Jill leaned forward suddenly to look up under the sail at Ben. She lost her balance, and then grabbed for the mast. The boat tipped wildly, and a big slurp of seawater rushed over the gunwale behind Ben.

"Sit back! Sit back!" Ben yelled. She did, and the boat evened up. "Grab that bailer and scoop the water out!"

Jill was sitting in four inches of slosh, but she didn't reach for the bailer. "You went into the school, and you didn't *tell* me?"

The wind gusted, and quickly they were thirty feet from the granite seawall in front of the school, closing fast.

"Ready about!" Ben yelled. "Duck!"

Jill ducked just in time and scrambled to the other side. When the wind caught the sail, the boat heeled up and all the water rushed her way again, splashing over her knees and legs.

Ben spoke quickly. "Just listen, okay? It was late, my mom was asleep, I had Mr. Keane's keys and I knew I could get in, so I went for it. That's all . . . sort of the way you rushed out Wednesday night and ripped up those surveying stakes—same kind of thing. And it seemed like a good idea, to have time to look around with no interruptions."

Jill reached for the bailer. Tossing scoop after scoop of water overboard, she scowled. "So you had to get one up on *me*, is that it?"

"No, that's *not* it," Ben said. "If I'd thought there was a way you could've gotten out last night, I'd have called you . . . except if I had, we'd have probably talked each other out of it. And I needed to *do* something."

Jill splashed half a scoop of salt water into his face. "Oops—I guess I'm not very *good* at this sailor stuff."

Ben blinked the water away and clenched his jaw. He set a course a few points off the wind, steering to reach a position south of the marina. He wanted to come about just once more and then run downwind, straight back to the beach. It was time for this voyage to end.

The boat skipped across the cold water, and the bow spray kept hitting Jill in the face, which was normal on a tack so close to the wind.

Ha—too bad!

But he was impressed that Jill didn't complain . . . or accuse him of making it happen on purpose.

After several minutes, she said, "So, you might as well tell me how it went at the school. Find anything?"

Ben was dreading this part too.

"No, not really. I was . . . interrupted."

Jill ducked low and looked up into his face. "You got *caught*?"

"Not actually caught. I was in the north stairwell, just getting started, and I got a text. All I can figure is, Lyman must have installed some kind of an alarm system in the last day or two. And we know he could have gotten hold of our cell phone numbers."

"A text from *Lyman*?"

"Well, the name was blocked, but it had to be

from him. It said, 'Go home now. At 12:09 your mommy wakes up.'"

"Your *mommy?*" Jill made a face. "*That* is creepy."

"Tell me about it. Then I got a phone call, and it was the Edgeport police. Which I didn't pick up. I sprinted home, and at exactly 12:09, my mom's phone rang. I'd just made it into bed, lying there sweating, and all she did was yell up the stairs to make sure I was okay. I have no idea if it was Lyman who called her, or what was said—probably, 'Sorry, wrong number,' or something. So, he won. And proved that he's got some skills."

"*Serious* skills," said Jill.

They were both quiet as the boat slapped along. Ben leaned forward a little and peeked at Jill's face through the plastic window in the sail. Her lips were blue, almost purple, and she was shivering. Below the sail he saw both her hands clenched tight—then he remembered the fresh cuts on her palms from pulling out those surveying stakes. The salt water had to sting like crazy.

"Sorry you got soaked," he said. "Not a very

nice introduction to sailing. I really wanted you to like it."

"Sailing?" she snapped. "Who says I don't like sailing? I just don't like you taking off on your own and being stupid."

"Oh, so yanking out a hundred stakes, that makes you a genius, right?"

She smirked. "At least when *I* did something dumb, I didn't get caught."

"Coming about!" he barked. "Duck!"

They scrambled to switch sides. The breeze had quartered toward the west, so Ben steered straight downwind at the beach north of the marina.

"Duck again."

He let the sheet out. The boom passed above Jill's head, and then he held it almost perpendicular to the hull. Now there was no sail blocking his view of her. She looked like a soggy puppy.

"Are you going to name your boat?" she asked. "I think you should call it *Brainless*."

He grinned across at her. "No, I'm gonna name it after you—*Grumpy Guts*."

"Very mature, Benjamin."

She acted annoyed, but he'd seen the tiny smile.

They were still about fifty yards from shore, and the water was already getting shallow. The breeze freshened, and the dinghy shot ahead.

"Look," he said, "we're coming in pretty fast, and I'm going to have to come about into the wind just before we hop out." Tapping with his free hand, he said, "This is the centerboard, and when I yell, 'Coming about,' pull it straight up, okay? And don't forget to duck."

Jill nodded meekly. The swell was running about two feet now, and the surf had kicked up. Again, the ocean demanded her respect.

It was easy to mess up a beach landing, and Ben didn't want to look like a total idiot . . . again. He scanned the next set of waves and spotted a lull, but he didn't really know this beach, so he had to guess about the depth.

Ten more yards, then, "Ready about!"

He hauled in the sheet, jammed the tiller to starboard, and the boat did a full one-eighty. Jill lifted the centerboard, and Ben hopped out into the water—right up to his waist. The sail flapped, and it took all his strength to keep the bow aimed into the wind. He backed toward the beach. As the first big wave hit the front of the boat, he lost his footing and his grip, and glugged all the way under.

Spluttering up, he grabbed the stern again, then pulled the rudder free of its pins and set it down in the well. Then he worked his way forward along the gunwale. Once he had hold of the bow, he backed the boat in toward the shore. Ben lowered the sprit, then said, "Help me lift it onto the sand, okay?"

"Sure," Jill said. She stepped into the water, and together they eased the boat up just beyond the waves.

While Ben got the sail down, Jill stood there shivering on the hard-pack, looking at one of the large yachts out past the piers. She cleared her throat loudly, and it seemed like she was forcing herself to speak. "It really was amazing to be out there . . . so thanks. And I'm sorry you think I'm such a . . . grump."

"No," he said quickly, "I deserved all that stuff you said. Listen, I can do everything else here, so you should go out to my dad's boat and get dried off—you look frozen."

"Actually, the sun feels warm now. I'll help."

"Great."

By the time they had the rigging off the boat, Ben's dad had come to the beach. He helped lift the hull up onto the dolly. The boat was only about eighty pounds, but it took all three of them to pull the dolly across the soft sand to the storage shed.

When the boat was stowed, his dad went to see Kevin at the security shed. Ben and Jill walked to the pier and climbed onto the planks.

She took off the borrowed waterproofs and hat and handed everything to Ben. Her lips weren't blue anymore, but she still looked like a wet puppy.

"So, if you can get over to the school by three thirty, I'll meet you at the back door by the loading dock. Okay?"

Ben nodded. "Sounds good . . . and thanks again for coming out with me."

"Thanks for asking. Maybe I'll get better at it."

"You did great for your first time—no kidding."

She rolled her eyes and smiled. "Right. I'll see you later."

"Yup, see you."

Her sneakers squished as she walked away. Ben chuckled to himself. Then he turned and headed out the pier toward the *Tempus Fugit*.

He took a quick inventory: a maiden voyage in his new sailboat, a rip-roaring argument at sea, a near capsize, *plus* an almost mutiny. And in an hour or so he'd meet up with Jill for more exploring at the school.

It was turning out to be quite a Saturday.

CHAPTER 5

The Weirdness Factor

"Hey—where are you guys?" The voice echoed down the long hallway.

Ben pulled Jill around the corner across from the library. "You *invited* him?" he whispered. "Why?"

They were on the first floor of the Oakes School. They had escaped the work party in the janitor's room by explaining to Jill's mom how they needed more photos for their history project.

From somewhere near the main office, Robert Gerritt called again.

"Hey, losers—Jill said we had to work on the project today, but if you're gonna play hide-and-seek, I'm outta here."

Jill started to answer, but Ben grabbed her arm and hissed, "Let him leave!"

She pulled free and went around the corner. "Down here, Robert—we were headed for the north stairwell. Sorry."

Turning back to Ben, she whispered, "I wanted him here because he's really smart, and we need him on our side."

Ben stared at her, his mouth wide open. "You don't mean . . ."

"Yes, that's *exactly* what I mean. We are running out of time here, Benjamin, so *I* say we tell him everything, and then—"

"Tell me what?"

Robert had a clipboard in one hand and a pocket video camera in the other. He aimed the camera Ben's way. "And speak up—this thing's got a lousy microphone."

Ben made a face and turned his back.

Jill said, "Well, it's kind of—"

"Ohhh," said Robert, wheeling to aim his video camera at Jill. "This is about how you two are all lovey-dovey now, right? Well, don't bother, okay? Besides it's all over the school anyway."

"What!?" Ben spun around, his face turning red. "That's just . . . that's *stupid*!"

Robert grinned, pointing his camera. "Oh, yeah . . . he's blushing—nice! Go on, you can talk about it . . . *Benjamin*. I can see you want to—and I'll try not to throw up. So come on, tell me *all* about it."

Standing there with clenched fists, Ben came close to wishing he'd let Robert drown last weekend.

"You're an idiot, Gerritt! We were talking about stuff you couldn't even *imagine*!"

Robert smirked. "Yeah, as if there's anything *you* could know that I didn't figure out two years ago—including how to sail better than you *ever* will! I am *so* glad I'm getting this on video!"

Ben stepped forward, and the two of them stood almost nose to nose.

"Okay," Ben growled, "here's something you *didn't* figure out"—he swatted Robert's arm away—"and shut off that stupid camera before *I* do it for you!"

Jill pushed her way between them. "Stop it, both of you!"

Robert clicked a button and held the camera

out so Ben could see the dark screen. "There, it's off, bigmouth. Finish what you were saying."

Ben kept his voice low, but he practically spat the words in Robert's face. *"You* think we're doing some stupid history assignment for a few extra-credit points! Well, we're *not*. There's a *war* going on here, and Jill and I are fighting to keep the school from being torn down. And even though there's a *spy* right here in these halls every day, we've already found gold and keys and secrets right under his nose, stuff that's been hidden since the 1700s! And *that's* what I didn't want to tell you, because you're a complete *zipperhead*!"

Robert looked at Ben a long moment, and glanced at Jill. Then he tipped his head back and laughed.

"Ha! You must *really* think I'm stupid if you think I'm gonna fall for *that*! Hidden gold? Secrets? *Spies?* Oooooh—scaaary! Is that the best you can do? Lame!"

Ben pulled out his phone and handed it to Robert. "Read this text, the one last night just after midnight—see it?"

"Yeah . . . so?"

"Follow me."

Ben turned on his heel and walked past the library, then took a right toward the northeast exit. Robert and Jill caught up to him.

"Last night I used the keys I got from Mr. Keane and I—"

"Hold it," Robert said, coming to a stop. "Old man Keane, the janitor? The dead guy? You've got *his* keys? *Right*."

Ben reached into his backpack, pulled out the keys, and shook them in front of Robert's face.

Ben was walking again. "Like I *said*, last night I opened *this* door, and minutes later I got *that* text on my phone. So right now, I need to look and see how the spy—that's right, Gerritt—how *the spy* knew that I was inside the school."

Ben pushed the door wide and began examining the outside edge.

"There!" Jill pointed. "Up there!"

Above the top hinge on the metal door jamb, there was a black rubber dot, no bigger than a penny.

Shrugging off his backpack as he pulled out his camera, Ben said, "Give me a boost up!"

Robert cupped Ben's foot.

After two quick pictures, Ben held the camera

out to Jill. "Here, and could you get me that ruler from my book bag? Thanks."

Using the flat end of the metal ruler like a spatula, he gently pried the dot off the door jamb, and then stepped down.

The three of them stared at the thing on the end of Ben's index finger.

"So . . . ," Robert said, "if what you told me is true, then someone stuck this sensor up there and closed the door on it. And when the door opened, that took the pressure off the sensor, which activated a tiny switch, and that sent a signal. I've heard about equipment that works like that . . . it all seems possible, I suppose. . . ."

Robert paused, his head tilted to one side.

"It's not just possible," Ben said triumphantly. "It's all *factual.*"

He felt like he'd just rubbed Robert's face in mud.

"So," Robert went on, "if this stuff *is* true, then *someone* is getting a signal that this door is standing wide open, *right now!*"

Robert grabbed the dot off Ben's finger and gently stuck it onto the paper on his clipboard. He pulled a dime out of his pocket and covered the dot with the coin. Flexing the spring-loaded jaw of the clipboard, he slid the paper until the dot and the dime were in position, then gently lowered the clip on them.

"There," he said. "The door's closed again!"

It took Ben a second or two to process everything Robert had done and said. He was pretty impressed, but he wasn't about to admit it. He just nodded and said, "Right," as if he would have done exactly the same thing.

Robert said, "So, are you two gonna to tell me the rest of what's going on here, or what?"

Ben looked at Jill, and she nodded at him.

"Well," Ben said, "I guess we *have* to now . . . but first you've got to swear an oath that you'll keep all this a secret—you can't tell anyone about any of it. At all. Okay?"

Robert grinned. "Ooh—a big secret oath! Sure thing . . . and then what? Do I get to sign my name in blood somewhere?"

Ben glared and started to reply, but Jill snapped faster, her voice edged with steel.

"Ben, I'm sorry. I *thought* Robert would understand what we're doing and want to help, but he *obviously* thinks that everything's a joke. You were right about him. He sails his fancy boat around and brags about winning races, but he couldn't care less about the bay or the town or anything. 'Sure, go ahead, rip down the school! And if the whole coast gets ruined, so what? Big joke—*ha ha ha*!'"

Robert was shocked by Jill's venom, and Ben used the moment. He grabbed the clipboard away and took the sensor and the dime off, pressing them tightly between his thumb and finger. He handed the clipboard back.

"We don't need you, Gerritt."

Jill wasn't done. "Just leave, Robert—*now*. And if you tell *anybody* what we've said about this, we'll find a way to get you back. We will. Let's go, Ben."

Ben started to leave, when suddenly everything seemed to slow down. Time slurred, and then almost stopped. It was like when he was ten, that instant when a buoy had smacked him in the mouth and chipped off both his front teeth. He saw every motion, each detail.

Jill's cheeks were flushed, her lips pressed together into a tight line, her eyes flashing angrily, her hands in tight little fists. She began to turn away.

Robert was stunned. His eyes jumped from Ben's face to Jill's. And as Ben watched it all in slow motion, that smug, sneering mask Robert had always worn crumbled—just dissolved, and then dropped away from his face. Ben saw real emotion in his eyes, and then, instantly, a fierce determination.

Robert spoke, but it was a changed voice. "Honest, guys—I didn't mean anything by that. You have to admit it, this whole thing? It seems completely crazy—it's really hard to believe, it is. Like . . . was I supposed to be ready for some big, serious swearing-in ceremony in the middle of a Saturday afternoon? I mean, c'mon. That was completely bizarre. But I see you're both really serious about this. I get it now—I do. So . . . yes—I swear that I will keep *all* of this a complete secret, everything. I want to be in on this, okay? Really, I *swear*."

His promise hung in the air.

Ben tapped his tongue against the back of his front teeth. He believed Robert. He almost felt a little sorry for the guy.

"Listen, Robert, I *know* this stuff sounds weird. And I also know I'm way too intense about all of it right now. But it *is* a big deal—a *huge* deal. And it doesn't just *seem* nuts, it really *is* nuts. I mean, you know Mr. Lyman, right, that tall janitor guy? Well, *he's* the spy, the one who's working for the theme park company. And that's the same guy who texted me—and *then* he called my house and woke up my *mom* in the middle of the night! So I *get* the weirdness factor. We threw all of this at you fast, but Jill's right, we really *do* need some help. So if you mean what you said, you're in." Ben put out his hand. "Shake on it?"

"Absolutely! Yeah, thanks!"

"And here," Ben said, holding out the sensor and the dime, "stick this back on your clipboard—

my wrist's about to break from squeezing so hard."

Jill shook his hand too. "Ben's right," she said. "We're both kind of insane about this right now. And I'm sorry I said some of that stuff—like, Ben didn't really say that about your sailing."

"Well," Ben said, "not out loud."

They all laughed a little at that, and it felt good to Ben—sort of. After all, he and Gerritt had a lot of history, most of it bad. This was the kid who had been teasing him, competing against him, constantly trying to show him up ever since first grade, both in school and now whenever their sailing club held a race. Still . . . Gerritt probably was about the smartest kid in the whole school, and to have him on their team might make a difference right now. Would it work out? Hard to say—but Ben knew one thing for sure. The team had to get down to work.

"So," he said to Robert, "there's a lot you need to know. First of all, back in 1791 Captain Oakes set up a group of kids he called 'The Keepers of the School'—that's from a message we discovered after Mr. Keane gave me this." He reached into his pocket and then handed Robert the smooth gold coin.

Robert read the inscription on each side, and Ben and Jill smiled as they watched his face. He was hooked.

During the next ten minutes Robert got the whole guided tour. They explained how that coin had been passed along from one janitor to the next for more than two centuries. They took him to see the secret hiding place "on the upper deck" and let him examine the big iron key and the list of safeguards. Then Jill showed him a copy of the codicil, the result of solving the "five bells" clue.

Robert was blown away. "So the Oakester actually *planned* all this? I mean, this thing with his will—it's *genius*! He laid out a big game of chess, and he's using *us* to play against his enemies—and if that codicil is for real, he wins! And he's been dead two hundred years! Incredible!"

They began walking down the south stairwell. "About that codicil," Jill said. "We talked to a lawyer, and she said we should only use it as a last resort."

"Yeah," Ben said, "because the Glennley people don't actually know what we're up to yet. And if we take that codicil to a judge, it would make the whole thing a huge public fight. Right now, it's still pretty much us against Lyman."

Robert looked at Ben. "So . . . yesterday afternoon, when you had me chase around the school and find Lyman because of that flood in the art room, that was part of this?"

Ben nodded. "I got detention on purpose, then I broke the faucet. I needed to search for something in the janitor's room, and I had to be sure Lyman wouldn't be there for a while."

"Did you find what you were looking for?"

"Yup. I met a man named Tom Benton at Mr. Keane's funeral, and he was the janitor here right before Mr. Keane. After I told him what was going on, he asked me to get him his old tackle box from the workshop. When I took it to him, turns out it was loaded with gold and silver coins—old, and really valuable. Mr. Keane had found them somewhere in the school and put them in the tackle box. So, as of yesterday afternoon, we have money in our treasury."

"Sweet!"

The three of them stopped on the landing between the first and second floor.

Robert cocked his head to one side a moment and narrowed his eyes. "Do you think Lyman knew there were going to be people from the

Historical Society here in the school today?"

"I'm sure he knew," said Jill. "When the school secretary came to let my mom in, she said she had to come herself because the janitor was out of town for the long weekend."

"Good," said Robert, "because *that* means we can go and disarm all the other doors, and if Lyman gets the signals before we put the squeeze on the sensors, he won't think it's weird that other doors were being opened."

"Actually . . . ," Ben said slowly, "*I* think we should let Lyman think that his system is still perfect." He pointed at the sensor on Robert's clipboard. "Let's get something small and black like that, and stick it back in the same place on the northeast door. The door'll still look like it's protected, but we'll be able to get in and out without setting off an alarm."

Robert nodded, and with a half smile he said, "I have to admit it, Pratt—that's a decent idea."

"How about we disarm one other exit and put up a fake sensor there, too," said Jill, "so we have a backup door? Maybe the exit on the south side of the Annex walkway?"

"*Another* decent idea," Robert said.

They walked down the last ten steps to the first-floor hallway near the office. The most direct route to the Annex causeway would have taken them past the janitor's room, so they went the long way around to avoid the grown-ups. But just as they got to the last corner near the art room—

"Jill? Can you hear me? We'd like some help carrying these tools now. Jill?"

"Coming, Mom."

They all changed direction.

"Well," Jill said, "we can fix that second door some other time. But maybe we can put up a fake sensor on that one door before we leave."

"Already got it figured out," said Ben. "Some black electrical tape and the scissors on my Swiss Army knife, and I'll be all set. I saw tape on the workroom bench yesterday."

"Nice," said Jill.

Walking into the janitor's room, Ben was sorry to see all the antique tools removed from their places on the wall. It was a great collection, close to a hundred different tools. They'd been protected by thick plastic cases, and now they were spread out all over the floor and the workbench.

He bent down and picked up a heavy block plane. The body of the thing was a solid chunk of bird's-eye maple. The iron was a little rusty, but it still looked plenty sharp. Someone had made this tool with great skill, taken good care of it, and used it hard for many years. It was like holding part of a person's life in his hands.

Ben's eye was drawn to some marks on the back end of the plane—two letters formed by holes punched into the wood: jv. Instantly Ben knew. He was holding one of John Vining's tools. He was the ship's carpenter who had sailed with Captain Oakes, and later he had drawn and designed every bookcase, every doorway, every bit of woodwork in the school. And then the master carpenter and his helpers had done the work themselves.

He took a quick look at a dozen other tools—they were all initialed.

"Hey," Ben said to Jill, "John Vining, the carpenter who made the drawings for the school construction? These are all his tools!"

Robert jumped in. "Vining? He's one of the people I'm featuring in my report—hey, we *are* still doing our reports for Mrs. Hinman, right? Because I don't want all my work on this stuff to go to waste."

"Of course we're doing our reports," Jill said. Lowering her voice, she asked, "So is there anything you know about Vining that might be useful for our *other* project? Vining must be the one who built all the hiding places for the safeguards. I've been meaning to go to the town library to do more research. Anything you can think of?"

"Hmm . . . not really. But I'll work on that."

"Can I have everyone's attention?"

A short man with white hair and a large nose stood at the doorway to the loading dock. "Please bring the tools out to my van one at a time, and use extra caution with the sharp ones. When everything's loaded, we can meet at the Historical Society building over on Bay Street."

As the kids and the other volunteers carried the tools out, the man arranged each one on a quilted moving pad until he ran out of space. Then he laid on a new pad and started a fresh layer. By the time they were almost done, there were nine layers.

Ben was glad everyone was so careful, but

he hated seeing the big blank space where the tools had hung for the past two hundred years. Although . . . they'd be right back there on the workroom wall in just a few weeks—if all went well.

That seemed like a very big "if."

Ben took the roll of electrical tape from the workbench and slipped it into his pocket. Then he excused himself to go use the washroom.

It took him only a few minutes to fashion a good replica of the door sensor—a small disk made from six circles of black vinyl tape. It was sticky on one side, smooth on the other. He walked around to the northeast door, opened it, stretched up on his toes, and pressed the black dot onto the same spot where the sensor had been. It looked perfect.

Back in the janitor's room, the job was done and the work party was breaking up.

"Hey, Ben, Jill," Robert said, loud enough for Jill's mom to hear. "How about we meet at the big beech tree tonight after dinner—maybe around seven? Toss a Frisbee around or play Wiffle ball? What do you think?"

"Can I, Mom?" Jill asked. "I'll be home before nine."

"I'll be walking home to the marina that way too," said Ben.

"Sure, that'll be fine," Mrs. Acton said. "Sounds like fun."

Robert caught Ben's eye, and Jill smiled at each of them.

As the man who owned the van removed the wooden wedge that had kept the loading dock door open, Ben spotted another small black sensor up high on the metal frame. The door wheezed shut, and he imagined Lyman getting a signal: All doors closed, locked up tight, safe and sound.

Ben hated to admit it, but he was impressed with Robert all over again. Meeting tonight for a game on the school grounds? That was brilliant.

Because they all knew they weren't going to be playing Wiffle ball—it was going to be more like hide-and-seek.

And Ben agreed with Jill's mom. It sounded like fun.

CHAPTER 6

Genius at Work

They sat on the low granite step in front of the northeast door of the school. They didn't look like burglars, just three kids eating Popsicles. But Ben was on high alert, noting every detail of their surroundings.

It was 7:35. Deep shadows stretched across the grounds of the school, but it was still fairly bright—and just seventy feet away, joggers and couples and small family groups strolled along the harborside walkway that passed in front of the school. Getting inside was going to be a challenge.

Ben held the one key he needed in his left hand—he'd removed it from the large key ring.

He finished his Popsicle, then casually stood up on the granite step and faced the door. Leaning in close, he pretended he was peering through the glass into the hallway, but both hands were busy. He unlocked the door, pulled it open half an inch, and slipped his Popsicle stick into the crack.

Ben sat back down on the step between Jill and Robert. The door was primed for action. Now it was just a matter of being patient, waiting for the right moment.

About five minutes later, it came.

A kid yelled out, "Hey, it's the big boat again!"

Ben got to his feet and stared, along with the dozen or so people out along the harbor walk. Bounding along on the strong easterly breeze, a three-masted schooner hove into view, flags and pennants flying. It was at least a hundred and fifty feet long, and Ben noticed it was Bermuda-rigged—one tall sail on each mast, plus two jibs hung from forestays running down to the bowsprit. It was a beautiful sight.

People clustered along the seawall, waving and calling out to the crew and passengers. Jill and Robert stood beside Ben, all of them caught up in the fun of the moment.

From fifty yards offshore the shrill notes of a bosun's pipe skittered across the water, and the schooner came about smartly. Taking the wind straight across her beam, the boat ran north along the shore, and a small wake curled off her bow. And that's when the mainsail came into full view.

Ben stopped smiling. Orange lettering marched across the broad canvas:

GLENNLEY
GROUP
PRESENTS

TALL
SHIPS
AHOY!

COME VISIT US
IN EDGEPORT
NEXT JUNE!
TALLSHIPSAHOY.COM

The three of them stood there, stunned and silent, while the sloop gathered speed.

"Okay," Ben said through his teeth. "Let's get to work."

As the crowd along the waterfront pointed and waved and cheered, the Keepers disappeared from the school's doorstep, Jill first, then Robert and Ben. They were all inside, and the door clicked shut.

"Hey, look!" said Robert, and he sprinted around the corner toward the library. "I'm running in the halls! Ha, ha—this is *great*!"

"Yeah," Ben called to him, "but we're here to *work*, so let's make a plan."

Robert sprinted back and screeched to a stop. "Listen," he said, panting, "before we get started, I had this really great idea, and I've got to go check something out—would that be okay?"

"Sure," said Ben, but he was sort of annoyed. This didn't seem like the new-and-improved Robert, the helpful, humble Robert, the one who had taken an oath a few hours ago. No, this was more like the

old Robert, the pushy one—the one who would just love to take over and run the whole show.

"Great!" said Robert. "So, do you think the janitor's room is unlocked? And if it's not open, do you have the key? I've got to look around in there."

"How come?" asked Jill.

"I was thinking some more about Lyman's alarm system."

"Yeah, what about it?" she said.

"You see, if there's a—"

Ben knew this feeling. It was like reaching for a race buoy out on the bay, only to have Robert come speeding in and steal all his wind. He felt like he needed to take charge.

"Okay, okay," Ben said, cutting Robert off, "let's just go see if the door's open instead of wasting time talking. Come on."

The door was locked, but Ben had all the other keys, and it only took a minute or so to find the right one.

The second he was in, Robert began walking slowly around the edge of the large room, examining the wall near the floor.

"Those door sensors? They're tiny, with tiny batteries and even smaller antennas. So there has to be something more powerful acting as a relay. I've got a pretty good idea about that, but *whatever* it is, it's probably plugged in, because it would have to be turned on all the time, ready to pick up a signal from one of the sensors. Also, batteries can lose power after a day or so, and this is a long weekend. And since this room is Lyman's home base in the school, the relay unit's probably in here. So we have to check out every electrical outlet and power strip in the room."

"All right, then," Ben said, "everybody look around." He wanted to be the one giving the orders.

Seconds later Jill called out, "Found something!"

Robert and Ben hurried over. A dark gray cord was plugged into a wall outlet behind the workbench. The cord ran upward, snaked onto the back edge of the bench, and ended at a six-outlet power strip, also dark gray.

Ben reached out to move some of the clutter concealing it, and Robert grabbed his arm. "Don't touch anything!"

Ben yanked his arm away. Gerritt was really getting on his nerves.

But he understood what Robert was thinking: If this *was* part of Lyman's alarm setup, it needed to look undisturbed.

Two small black transformers were plugged into the power strip. The thin black cord from each transformer led to a rumpled stack of blue shop rags near the end of the bench closest to the loading dock.

Robert carefully peeled back half the stack of rags. "Yup," he said, "just like I thought."

One of the cords ran into a slim black box about the size of a TV remote. A row of red LED lights flicked on and off in sequence—left to right, then back again, a constant wave of tiny blinks. Two silver wires about an inch long stuck up from the oblong box, one at each end.

Robert pointed at the wires. "Antennas. One of them probably picks up the signal from a door sensor. Then the processor in the box decodes which door the signal came from, and then the other antenna sends that information to *this*."

Lifting up one last shop rag, Robert revealed an ordinary-looking cell phone. It was flipped open and the small LCD screen was dimmed, showing only the time stamp—7:43 p.m.

"So," Ben said, "a sensor sends a blip, the box decodes it, sends a signal that wakes up that phone, then the phone dials a preprogrammed number, and the information zips to Lyman. Sweet and simple."

"Yeah . . . ," Robert said. "I would have explained it better, but that's basically it."

Ben nodded wisely, staring at the blinking red lights, trying to think of something else to say, something that sounded *really* smart.

He couldn't think of a thing—nothing at all.

Then he had a sudden, terrible realization: *I'm faking it!*

And he was, completely. He was acting like he'd had this whole thing figured out from the start. And he really hadn't. None of this stuff would have *ever* occurred to him, not in a million years.

So, what? Am I trying to win some big contest here? A game of Who's the Smartest?

Ben's next thought was even worse.

Agghh! I've turned into Gerritt—I really have!

He felt embarrassed, like he'd just been caught in a total lie. He even felt himself starting to blush.

Ben glanced at Jill—she was looking right at him, a puzzled expression on her face.

She knows too! Jill knows that I'm trying to out-Robert Robert!

The horror of that idea snapped Ben's mind into total clarity. He realized instantly that there was only one possible way out of this mess.

Ben looked Robert full in the face and gave him an honest smile, no pretending. "This is amazing, Gerritt—really, just incredible!"

His compliment took Robert by surprise. Flustered and clearly pleased, he mumbled, "Um . . . thanks a lot."

But Robert's humility attack ended quickly.

"Well, if you think *that* stuff is cool, check *this* out!" He pulled a phone from his back pocket. "Do you know what *this* is?"

"Duh," said Jill. "Could it be . . . a *cell phone*?"

Robert ignored her sarcasm. "I *knew* you wouldn't know. It's *not* a regular cell phone—it's a ghost phone. I was pretty sure we'd find a phone in here, so I went to CVS this afternoon, and they had a whole rack of prepaid phones—no plans to buy, no credit cards, no ID needed. I took this one up to the register and bought it, just like that—nine dollars and ninety-four cents—which includes twenty minutes of talk, plus texting. I can walk into a store and buy more minutes with cash anytime I want. And if I text or call somebody, *no one* can trace who the call is from. Pretty cool, huh?"

Jill looked at Robert blankly. "And the *purpose* is . . . ?"

Robert grinned and looked at Ben. "How about you, Pratt? See where I'm going with this?"

"Not a clue," Ben said cheerfully. He was actually looking forward to being amazed again.

Robert laughed, enjoying his own show. "Okay, watch carefully."

He pushed a little catch on the back of his new phone and popped out the battery. Inside the battery compartment, he moved a small metal band to one side and lifted out a thin green-and-gold wafer.

"You *must* know what this is, right?"

Jill nodded. "That's a SIM card—it's the phone's memory."

"Yes," Robert said, "but you only get *half* credit. Because even with its SIM card removed, there's still *some* memory in the electronics of the phone itself—and that's important."

He picked up Lyman's phone from the pile of rags and unplugged the power cord.

"Hey!" said Ben. "Won't Lyman know?"

Robert held out the phone. "See the display? Just the time. If it's not showing a phone number, it can't send a signal."

In five seconds he had shut it down and removed the battery and the SIM card from Lyman's phone as well.

"Now, *this* is the beautiful part." He fiddled with the phone pieces and punched buttons as he talked. "I plug Lyman's SIM card into my ghost phone . . . I put my battery back in, then turn on the phone . . . okay. Now, I access my menu, and I tell it to copy all of *Lyman's* information into *my* phone's internal memory . . . and, it's starting . . . halfway there . . . and all done! Whatever he had on his phone, it's now on *mine*! Now I shut my phone down . . . battery out, then Lyman's SIM goes back into *his* phone, then his battery . . . I turn it on, plug it back in, put it down, cover everything up again . . . and it's like we've never been here! Then *my* SIM goes back into the ghost phone . . . then the battery . . . then we close it up and turn it on. And now, we can take our time and look through my phone and see *all* of Lyman's numbers and contacts. And if we decide to make any calls to his contacts, no one will know who called. Now, of course, we might not have any new data at all. If I was Lyman, I'd have hidden a ghost phone here in the workroom—with nothing on the SIM card except one other dead-end number. Of course, it's entirely possible that Lyman's not as smart as me."

"Um . . . ," said Jill, "I think that should be 'as smart as *I.*'"

"What? Oh . . . right, as smart as *I* am." Robert smiled, unruffled by the grammar correction. "So, you guys have any questions before we take a look at the captured data?"

Ben was surprised that Jill seemed to be looking for faults at this moment—but then again, when Robert went full-on about how wonderful he was, it could be pretty awful . . . maybe he was just more used to dealing with it. At any rate, Ben wanted to give Gerritt full credit for some terrific thinking.

"That is just *fantastic!*" said Ben, and he let the compliment hang in the air a moment. "However, right *now*, it's almost eight o'clock. How about we use our time here in the building to look for the next safeguard—does that make sense?"

"Sure," Robert said, and Jill nodded.

So Ben said, "Great. Gerritt, I can't wait to see what was on Lyman's phone, but could you look through all of it on your own later, and maybe make up a list of whatever was there? Then we can really study it and see if there's a way to use it."

"Sure," said Robert, "that'll work. No problem."

"Great—really, that whole phone thing? Totally amazing." Ben was already walking. "Pull the workroom door shut, okay, Jill? Now, if we get over into the north stairwell, I can show you what I was doing there last night—before Lyman interrupted me. I want to see what you guys think."

It was very dark inside the north stairwell, and Ben and Jill turned on the small flashlights they'd brought.

"Hey," said Robert, "can you two maybe share a flashlight? I didn't bring one."

Ben resisted the temptation to say something about how some people maybe weren't quite as smart as they seemed to be—something he definitely would have said a day ago. The competition thing was a bad habit. "Sure—here," and he handed Robert his flashlight.

Ben counted up to the seventeenth tread, and then asked Jill and Robert to examine it. They did, and each came to the same conclusion he had—there was nothing odd about it.

Then, starting over again from the first landing, they counted up *another* seventeen treads, which put them near the middle of the flight that began on the second floor. Again, there was nothing unusual about *that* seventeenth tread.

"You know, we've actually got to look at every single step above the first seventeenth," Robert observed, "'cause, really, you can start counting up seventeen treads from almost anywhere—if you get what I mean."

Jill and Ben agreed, so that's what they did. It took them almost twenty minutes to examine every possible seventeenth tread from the first floor up to the third. Then they all walked around to the south stairwell and repeated the whole long process again.

Ben found that he liked having all three of them there hunting together—so much more fun than trying to do this alone in the middle of the night. And Robert was just plain *smart*—Ben had no problem admitting that to himself. Jill had made a good call, bringing him onboard . . . not that he wasn't still annoying. . . .

But I suppose *I* can be annoying too, he thought.

Anyway, it felt like having Robert around was probably going to work.

After finding nothing in the south stairwell, they all walked through the third-floor hallway back to the north stairwell. Ben followed Jill, and they started down.

"Hey, guys?" Robert called.

Ben and Jill looked up from the flight below him. He was standing still, three steps down from the third-floor landing, his head cocked slightly to one side. "I *think* I just figured something out."

Jill looked at Ben, and he read her face: *Oh boy, here he goes again.* But they both smiled a little and shrugged. After all, Gerritt had had some pretty amazing ideas so far.

Besides, they both knew it really didn't matter whether they wanted to hear what he had to say or not.

Robert was going to tell them anyway.

CHAPTER 7

Recount

"We've been going at this all wrong, I'm sure of it!"

Ben and Jill walked up to where Robert was. He stood above them like a professor in a lecture hall, ready to give his presentation.

"The clue says, 'After four times four, tread up one more.' Now, based on how I think the captain chose his words in the first clue, and supported by the actual solution you two worked out, the words of *this* clue suggest to me that we *are* in the right area—I'm almost positive we're supposed to be hunting here in the stairwells. But we are *not* supposed to be counting steps. We *should* be counting"—and Robert paused dramatically—"*these!*"

He ran his hand back and forth across four or

five balusters, the wooden posts holding up the handrail. He looked like he was playing a harp.

Ben did the math out loud. "Four times four *balusters*, that would mean going up eight steps, then 'tread up one more' to the ninth step. So we're looking for the seventeenth *baluster*—or possibly the eighteenth, which would also be on tread number nine! Let's go!"

It was a miracle no one died during the race down to the first floor.

Jill got there first. "Look," she said to Ben, "you've got to adjust for this."

They hadn't counted on the large support at the end of the railing—which meant that the first step only had one baluster.

Robert narrowed his eyes. "*I* think Captain Oakes would have included the newel post as one of the first sixteen—anyone want to bet?"

Ben grinned and shook his head. "Not me." He'd become a true believer. Robert really *was* a genius, or at the very least, he had an amazing gift for spotting little details, the stuff that really mattered . . . maybe that was what being a genius meant. But Ben didn't really care. At that moment, he was ready to take out a full-page ad in the *Boston Globe*:

ROBERT GERRITT IS A GENIUS!

Jill didn't want to bet against Robert either. She'd already followed him back up to the ninth step.

Using the end of Ben's flashlight, Robert started tapping on the balusters—first the one closest to the edge of step number nine, then the one at the back, then three or four on the other steps above and below.

"Hear the difference?" he whispered excitedly.

He tapped each piece of wood again. All but one made a deep, solid *thunk*. The rear baluster on step nine sounded different—it made a higher tone, more of a *plink*, and there was a tiny buzz, a vibration.

Jill said, "Try turning it."

Robert looked at Ben. "Should I?"

"Sure, why not?"

"Well . . . which way should I twist? I don't want to break anything."

Ben shrugged. "Try counterclockwise—righty-tighty, lefty-loosey, that's how things usually work. Just go easy in case something starts to crack."

"Hold this," Robert said to Jill, and he handed her Ben's flashlight.

He gripped the narrowest parts of the baluster, one hand near the railing and the other down close to the tread. "Here goes . . . ," and he took a deep breath.

Ben saw Robert's arm muscles tense, saw his knuckles turn white. He began breathing again, and his face went bright red as he strained.

"I can feel . . . some give . . . but it's not . . . turning."

"Let me help," said Jill. She set her flashlight down and reached between Robert's arms, grabbing the rounded center of the baluster with both hands.

"Me too!" Ben hurried up and got a grip just above and below Robert's hands. "Okay, on the count of three—one, two, *turn*!"

Ben felt a little movement. "Give it all you've got!"

Robert grunted with effort and Jill made a high-pitched "Mmmmmmmmmm!"

Almost laughing, Ben let out a long "YaaaaaaahhhhHHHH!"

As their battle cries hit a wild crescendo, the baluster twisted ninety degrees—*kanonk!*

"All *right!*" They laughed and slapped high fives all around.

Then Ben held up his hand. "But . . . what just happened, like, what did that *do*?"

"Well," Robert said, "if my theory's correct, we need to look below—can I use one of the lights again?"

They hurried down to the stairwell floor. Robert aimed a flashlight back past the newel post, lighting up the paneled woodwork of the wall running alongside the staircase.

"I never noticed this area before, did you, Ben?"

"Nope, not really."

Ben shined his flashlight up at the twisted baluster on step nine, then brought the beam straight down. "Hey!"

Robert said, "I see it too!"

Jill stepped forward and put her hand onto the woodwork where the two flashlight beams met. "There's a crack . . . and it runs all the way down to the point." She dropped to her knees. "And if I can get my fingers around the end here . . ."

She gripped the edges of the wood and pulled. Silently, two sections of the paneling swung outward as a single unit, a large triangular door.

"That is *awesome*!" whispered Robert.

Ben was already at the opening, his camera aimed back into the area under the steps. A sharp, acrid smell hit his nostrils, but he ignored it and snapped a picture. The flash temporarily blinded him, but he aimed again and took another shot, changing the angle.

"I always take photos—," he began, but Robert cut him off.

"Right—documentation, placement of artifacts, site integrity—I get it."

"Shhh!" Jill whispered. "Did you hear that?"

Ben crouched down and looked into the opening, but his eyes were still flash-blind. Then he heard it too. And he knew what it was.

Jill peered over his shoulder.

"It's a rat, a rat!"

She backed away and flattened herself against the wall.

Ben shined his light into the opening. Just two

feet away a large Norway rat stood halfway up on its hind legs, eyes reflecting red, ears and whiskers twitching. It didn't seem particularly concerned about the visitors.

But when Robert clapped his hands, the rat skittered away. There was a lot of movement off in the darkness.

"They won't be a problem," Robert said. "Rats're incredibly smart—they've got to have a way out of there, probably already left. C'mon, I'll go in first."

Jill stayed put. "Not me . . . no way."

"Listen," Ben said, holding up a hand. "I think they're gone."

Robert leaned low, his hands on the baseboard.

It was completely still. Then suddenly, *vreet, vreet, vreet!*

Jill jumped a foot, and Robert jerked his hands back like he'd been shocked.

Ben had to laugh. "Sorry—it's my phone. I set an alarm for eight forty-five. We've got to leave."

"Leave *now*? Are you kidding?" said Robert.

"I know it stinks," Ben said, "but I've really got to be home by nine."

Jill nodded eagerly. "Me too."

Ben resisted teasing her about the rats. He looked at Robert. "Really, I'm sorry to leave when we're so close here, but I promised my dad I'd be home on time—we've got to set up at dawn tomorrow. I mean, I guess you could stay and look around on your own. . . ."

Robert hesitated, as if he just might do that. But he shrugged and said, "Nah, that's okay. I can wait." He turned and trotted up to the ninth stair. "You two shove on that door, and I'll lock it into place."

They pushed, and as Robert turned the baluster, he said, "It moves a lot easier now."

The three of them left the stairwell and hurried to the northeast door. Ben took a peek. It was almost dark outside. A few people were on the harbor walk, but they were well north of the school.

"All clear," he said, and pushed the door open.

They walked over to the seawall. After the dark stuffiness of the stairwell, the ocean breeze was like a cool drink.

"So . . . what?" Robert said. "How about we come back tomorrow night—same time, same place."

Jill shook her head. "We're going to a family reunion in New Hampshire. I won't get back till late Monday."

"Yeah," Ben said. "I'm away too. My dad and I are sailing down to Plymouth, unless the forecast changes."

"You doing anything this weekend?" Jill asked Robert.

"Oh, yeah," he said, "you know, tons of family stuff. Well, I should get going too. Guess I'll see you Tuesday." He hesitated a moment, looking out across the water. "Listen, thanks for letting me in on all of this. I owe you—both of you."

"I'm glad you joined up," said Jill.

"Me too," Ben said. "We made lots of progress, and you really helped."

"Thanks. Well, I'm going thataway," and he pointed west.

Jill smiled. "See you Tuesday."

"Oh," Robert said, "and if there's anything really cool on Lyman's phone, I'll text you."

"Great," Ben said, "except I won't get any messages till I get home. When we take the boat out, it's no-phones-allowed. But send stuff anyway, okay?"

"Will do," and Robert set off on the path that cut through the grounds toward School Street.

Jill and Ben walked south along the shoreline. Ben saw the lights of a dozen or so small craft out on the bay, and close in, a big yacht with furled sails motored toward the harbor, its green and red running lamps swinging fore and aft. Little *clanks* and *bongs* drifted in from the bell buoy at Buzzard's Rock, two miles away. It was cool and calm, a perfect night for walking. And thinking.

Except the thinking ruined the walk.

Ben kept wondering, What if we fail? By *next* May, construction work on the theme park would be almost done, counting down to their huge grand opening. Memorial Day weekend on Barclay Bay would never be like this again, not ever. If they failed.

Jill must have been worrying too. Crossing Adams Street, she said, "I think having Robert around improves our chances, don't you?"

"Absolutely," Ben said. "And just so it's out of

the way once and for all, you were right about him, and I was wrong."

She looked sideways and smiled. "Please, say that last part again, only slower, and with feeling."

He laughed, then stretched out both arms like an opera singer and cut loose. "And *I* was *wrooooong*! How's that?"

"Sweet!"

"Well, I'm glad you enjoyed it—because it's entirely possible I will *never* need to say that again."

"Yeah, right—in your dreams!"

They stopped at the corner of Jefferson Street. Jill's family lived in a condo building just uphill from the harbor walk.

"I'm actually sort of proud of you, Benjamin."

Ben snorted. "Yeah? And what's the punch line?"

"I'm not joking," she said. "I saw what you did, when the three of us were there in the workroom tonight."

"What?" he said.

But Ben knew what she was talking about.

"It was when Robert was doing his high-tech

show with the phones. Right in the middle of it, you stopped trying to be the big chief. You let *him* be the smart guy—even though he's *completely* conceited most of the time. That was nice."

Ben felt a blush climbing up his neck. He was glad it was almost dark.

He swallowed hard. "I—I was just telling the truth. That guy has to be some kind of genius, y'know."

"Yes," she said, "but what you said and the way you said it, I could tell it meant a lot to him. I think he's been jealous of you for a long time."

"Gerritt?" Ben snorted. "What're you talking about? Why would he be jealous of *me?*"

"Lots of reasons," said Jill. "For example, last Saturday? If it had been *you* who'd flipped a boat over, would *he* have jumped into the water to save you? I think Robert wonders about that. I know *I* do. . . ."

Ben didn't like the way this conversation was going. Steering it back to what had happened at the school, he said, "Well, anyway, I'm glad I told him how impressed I was with that cell phone stuff. And you're right, I think it meant something to him. Did you see his face, when I said that?"

Jill shook her head. "I wasn't looking at his face. I was looking at yours."

Then she said, "Good night, Benjamin. Have fun sailing with your dad . . . and when he yells, 'Ready about!' be sure to duck."

"Right. See you Tuesday."

CHAPTER 8

The High Ground

"Did you remember to duck?"

"What?" said Ben. "Oh—right, coming about. Yeah, I ducked every single time, see?" He pointed at his head. "No bumps, no bruises."

"Good. Although"—Jill paused and smiled—"a good whack on the head might be what you need, knock some sense into you."

"Yes . . . but what if I *hadn't* ducked, and that whack on the head had made me even crazier? Think of my poor dad, stuck on a small sailboat with a crazy person."

"Right." Jill nodded. "I know how *that* feels."

Ben laughed and shook his head. "So, what?

You've turned into a comedian now? I miss the good old days when all you did was snap and snarl and yell at me."

Jill narrowed her eyes. "Watch your step, Pratt—those days could come back any second."

They'd reached the corner of Haddon Lane. It was Tuesday morning, another perfect spring day—the fourth one in a row. All around them other kids were also headed for school, and everyone was walking as slowly as possible. The long weekend had been a sweet taste of summer vacation—wonderful, but cruel. Nobody wanted to go back.

When he and Jill had met up to walk to school, she'd told him about her family reunion up at Lake Winnipesaukee. Then he'd told her a little about his sailing trip down to Plymouth. Ben felt like he'd been away for a month—a welcome break from his life onshore, and an *especially* welcome break from Captain Oakes and his school.

Still, as much fun as the sailing had been, he'd been aware every second that his mom wasn't onboard. He felt pretty sure his dad had noticed too.

Not that they'd talked about that. They hadn't

really talked much at all. Both down the coast and back, it had seemed more like March than May—a fifteen-to-twenty-knot easterly wind, with a two-to-three-foot swell. The sailing had been intense, and the *Tempus Fugit* had lived up to her name—they'd flown.

By dusk on Sunday they had anchored in Duxbury Bay just north of Clark's Island. After squaring away, they'd had supper onboard and then dropped into their bunks, exhausted. They'd talked a little, but mostly about the boat and the rigging and the weather—sailor talk. Nothing personal. Nothing about the family. Nothing about Mom.

And that made Ben wonder how things were between Jill's parents. Her mom was totally against the new amusement park, and her dad, a businessman, had just bought two thousand shares of stock in the Glennley Group. He knew Jill was worried . . . maybe he should ask her about it.

But Ben was glad when Jill picked up the conversation and took it in a completely different direction.

"Did you read Robert's text about all the names and numbers he found on Lyman's phone?"

Ben nodded. "First thing I did when we got back to the marina. Pretty amazing. I bet we can figure out who a lot of those contacts are, and we might be able to use that stuff somehow—maybe to distract Lyman or something. I can't wait to see the printouts Gerritt made."

"Yeah, me either."

They crossed Washington Street, and as they walked onto the school grounds, Ben stopped short and pointed. "Look—the stakes are gone again! Did you . . ."

Jill held out her palms for inspection. "I'm innocent. Actually, the school board had all of them removed last Friday—didn't you hear about that? They were afraid kids would run into them and get hurt, which would mean lawsuits. No more surveying stakes until the construction fences go up."

"Which means no more stakes *ever*," added Ben, "if we do our job."

"Speaking of our job, there's Robert. I guess he got the text you sent him last night. Look, he's pretending we don't exist. He's not a very good actor."

It was true. Robert was walking their way,

heading toward the front door. He was working very hard to look like he wasn't paying any attention to either of them. Ben smiled and looked away.

He had sent Robert a simple text late Saturday night:

> Don't hang out with Jill and me at schl.
> Ur the keepers secret weapon.

Robert had replied instantly.

> Got it—stealth bomber

Ben looked up as he went in the front door. On the door frame to the left, he saw one of Lyman's little black sensors. The enemy was close. Lyman was already inside somewhere, actively opposing them.

Even so, Ben felt good as the three of them walked into the front hallway together. If they could keep Lyman in the dark about Robert, it would help level the playing field. Actually . . . it might be more like taking control of the high ground during a battle.

Ben and Jill turned left at the office. She had homeroom on the third floor, and he had to go up there and get something from his locker. Ben glanced over his shoulder and spotted Robert. He was walking the other direction, headed for the north stairwell. His homeroom was on the third floor too, but he was clearly trying to avoid being anywhere near them—probably afraid he might blow his cover. Ben smiled to himself. Seemed a little silly to take things that far. But then again, there was nothing silly at all about controlling the high ground. Because every day from now on was going to be a battle.

Controlling the high ground . . . it was a concept that he had learned during his very first snowball fight. Being up higher *mattered*.

There was heavy traffic in the south stairwell, and as he trudged slowly upward, Ben thought about that.

He had never really *studied* warfare, but he'd read about plenty of historical battles, both on land and at sea. Out at sea, there *was* no high ground. Sailing on the wide ocean, the old warships won battles by being larger, faster, and having bigger cannons. Even then, it was tough to get an advantage. Sometimes you could sneak up on an enemy ship at night or through a fog, but usually an opponent saw you coming from miles away. To win, you had to outsail the other captain, get into firing position, and shoot *your* cannons first—*BOOM!*

A land battle was very different, and controlling the high ground was vital. Gravity was a powerful force. From up above, your cannons could fire a *lot* farther than your enemy's. But controlling the high ground didn't guarantee a victory—you still had to be smarter or stronger or better prepared, and it helped to be all three.

Back in October he'd done a social studies report on the Battle of Bunker Hill. The story had made a strong impression on him.

In June of 1775, Boston was under siege. British ships controlled the harbor, pounding the city with their cannons. Then English generals ordered soldiers to land and take control of some high ground by the harbor—Breed's Hill and Bunker Hill.

But patriot spies heard about the attack, and the Americans rushed to the top of Breed's Hill first. There were about seven hundred men with no training, lousy weapons, and not enough ammunition. They dug ditches and put up low walls of dirt.

Two thousand Redcoats started marching up the hill. They thought the rebels would just run away some of the British didn't even load their rifles. An American officer gave that famous order: "Don't fire till you see the whites of their eyes!"

The British got closer, and the colonists waited and waited—and then fired. They made every shot count.

However, the British attacked three times, and the high ground didn't save the colonists. They retreated from the top of Breed's Hill, and American casualties were bad—140 killed, and more than 300 wounded. But British losses were *huge*, the most soldiers lost during any single battle of the whole Revolutionary War: 226 dead and 828 wounded.

Those terrible losses made the British change their plans about taking control of Dorchester Heights—which was the *really* important high ground above Boston. And several months later, who took command of the Heights? General George Washington—and then *American* cannons started pounding the British. The patriots pushed the English completely out of Boston, and finally went on to win the whole war.

Ben counted off the last five steps up to the landing. Winning America's independence hadn't been easy. And *this* war, today? At the moment, he felt outnumbered and outgunned. Victory seemed a long way off.

When they came out of the stairwell onto the third floor, Jill said, "You're dangerously quiet all of a sudden—what're you thinking about?"

Ben shrugged. "Warfare, tactics, espionage, casualties—fun stuff like that."

He stopped at his locker and began dialing the combination.

"Do you have a plan for today?" Jill asked.

He nodded. "Yup. I plan to eat two pieces of chocolate cake at lunch. And we've *also* got to come up with a way to check out that new space."

"You mean, the rathole?" said Jill.

Ben smiled as he pulled the locker open. "Yeah, that's what I—"

The next word stuck in his throat. He stared, his eyes wide.

"What?" said Jill. She moved and looked over his shoulder.

A scrap of paper was taped onto the inside of the metal door, a note scrawled in pencil:

Not bad—for an amateur

Ben wasn't looking at the note. He was looking at the tape. The paper was stuck to the locker door with black electrical tape, six pieces of it, and each piece was a circle about as big as a penny. He pointed at one.

"Lyman found the fake sensor."

"I don't care *what* he found!" Jill hissed. "Nothing

gives him the right to open your locker—you have to report this!"

Ben pulled out his little camera and snapped a picture of the note. Then he reached into his locker, got a book of Jack London stories, and slapped the door shut.

"You're just *leaving* it there?" she said.

He nodded grimly. "To remind us what we're up against. Keep thinking about our next moves, okay? Especially since he knows we're onto his alarm system. See you in math."

Ben walked off quickly before Jill could study his face.

He went down the long hall, past the compass

rose, past the tall portrait of Captain Oakes, past the cache where they'd found the big key and the list of safeguards. He turned the corner and hurried into the north stairwell—and there was Lyman on the third-floor landing, tall and thin, leaning on the handle of a dust mop. When he saw Ben, his long face broke into a crooked smile.

Ben rushed past him onto the stairs, taking the first flight two at a time.

"Whoa there, young fella," Lyman called out, "easy on those steps. It's gonna be summer real soon—be a shame to start it in a plaster cast."

Ben gave the man a dirty look as he rounded the next newel post. He slowed down, but not much.

Ben was glad the kids around him couldn't read his mind, and he was glad

Jill wasn't there—she would have seen the rage. With each step down and down, his thoughts got bloodier.

You scum-bucket! You wanna play dirty, is that it, Lyman? Open my locker and grub through my stuff? How about I slash all the tires on your truck—and break your windshield, too? And after you get the windshield fixed? A big can of white paint, right through the glass! And listen up, *creep*—I know where you live. Stuff's gonna happen over there! Rocks through the windows, dog poop on the front steps, and in your mailbox? Rotten eggs, dead fish, squashed skunks—*surprise*! And I almost forgot, *smart guy*—we captured your cell phone! So get ready for round-the-clock bombardment! 'Cause now *I'm* gonna call *your* mommy at Sun City in Arizona, and I'm gonna call her at *three in the morning* every day until she has to get a new phone number. How's *that?* And I'm gonna prank-call your boss, and your boss's boss, and your boss's boss's boss! You messed with the wrong kid, *dirtbag*—and now it's *war!*

He was on the last flight down to the first floor, and Ben realized his hand was hurting—it was clenched in his front pocket, gripping the big gold coin so tightly that his fingers had cramped up.

The words on the coin jumped into Ben's thoughts: *First and always, my school belongs to the children: Defend it!*

Defend . . .

That one small word pulled Ben back to himself.

Did the coin say, *Destroy any dirtbag who dares to attack my school*?

No. It said, *Defend* the school.

And Captain Oakes had laid out the plan: Find the safeguards, and use them for *defense*. His plan did *not* authorize personal attacks. This was supposed to be a civilized process.

Right now the war was going their way, and he and Jill and Robert had control of the high ground. Ben felt sure about that. And if they were smart and careful, they could *hold* that ground.

Rounding the corner near his homeroom, he let out a deep sigh—mostly relief, but a touch of disappointment, too. Because part of him would have *loved* going after Lyman—loading up, aiming, and then blasting him right out of town.

But the captain's way had to be better. If the Keepers had to turn into people like Lyman in order to win, that would mean giving up a different kind of high ground. Yes, they needed to win this war, but not by turning into thugs.

The war was under way, and the enemy forces were already marching up the hill. But they could build a strong defense—*if* they got all their safeguards into place.

Ben knew what they had to do. Because if the Keepers started the final battle too soon, the enemy would overpower them. Now was the time for courage, hard work, and especially patience— "Don't fire till you see the whites of their eyes!"

CHAPTER 9

Inner Space

"Ewww!"

"Shhh!" Ben whispered.

"I heard rats! And the smell . . ."

"Either shut up, or get out—what's it gonna be?"

"I'll be quiet . . . I promise."

"Keep your light on, and the rats won't come near you."

Only minutes earlier it had looked like Tuesday would *not* be the day they explored under the stairs. Lyman had kept a close watch on Jill and Ben all day long, and Robert the Stealth Bomber had not volunteered for a solo mission into the darkness. Patience still seemed like the wisest option.

As usual, they had set up their study areas in the library right after school—Ben and Jill in the alcove on the north wall, and Robert off by himself at a table near the American history section.

And, as usual, Lyman had stopped in to check on Ben and Jill—except today he hadn't even bothered to act like a janitor. He'd just walked in, stared at them, frowned, and then left.

The second he had gone, Robert rushed to the alcove. "Listen up," he whispered. "In eight minutes you two go to the north stairwell and check out that space, okay? You can only stay *ten* minutes, then come right back here."

"What?" said Ben. "We don't—"

"Listen—I've got a diversion, I planned it all weekend. Exactly *eight* minutes from my mark, okay?"

"A diversion? What—"

Robert shook his head. "No time!" He looked at his watch. "Eight minutes . . . from *now*! Trust me!"

And with that, Robert had rushed out of the library, waving at Mrs. Sinclair and saying, "Have to go to the restroom!"

Jill and Ben had decided to trust him—which

was why they were standing just inside the area under the steps.

Getting in had been easy today—the baluster turned smoothly, the triangular panel had swung open noiselessly, and they had crouched low and stepped inside, Ben first.

And now with the door pulled shut behind them, he spotted a hook made of hammered iron that was clearly meant for holding it closed. With camera in one hand and flashlight in the other, Ben turned around.

He didn't really like having to be the brave one here, didn't like having to be the one knocking down all the spiderwebs and taking the first few steps on the crunchy floor. But Jill, usually so fearless, was totally unnerved by the rats. She clung to her small light like it was the last life vest from the *Titanic*.

She was right about the smell. It reminded him of the odor from the bats in his grandparents' shed up in Maine. Rat droppings, bat droppings—pretty much the same.

John Vining had done nice finish work in the little room, and Ben admired the carpentry. The walls were covered in pine boards with hardly a hairsbreadth between them. The slanted ceiling of the stairs rising above them was also layered with pine. From the highest point of the slant, a sooty brass lantern hung from a chain hooked to a nail.

It was easy for Ben to imagine lots of uses for this room back when Captain Oakes had his shipping business—especially when the British began taxing everything going to and from the colonies. This would have been a perfect place to hide chests of tea, bolts of silk, or barrels of molasses— also a safe spot for bags of gold or silver coin.

Jill was right behind him, almost stepping on his heels. "Any rats?"

"*Shh*—no!"

He shined his light straight ahead—a door, slightly ajar! He'd expected to see the area there to his left, the space directly below the landing, but a door? Leading where? The pictures he'd snapped Saturday night hadn't shown that.

Ben pulled an index card and a pencil from his pocket, and holding the flashlight in his mouth, he made a quick sketch that showed the layout of the space.

"Look!" Jill was shining her light elsewhere, and Ben swung around.

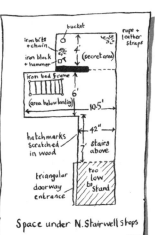

On the board next to the triangular door through which they had entered, someone had scratched tally marks into the wood.

"Sixty-seven," she whispered.

"Shut your eyes," said Ben, aiming his camera.

He did the same and snapped a photo of the marks. Then he turned around again, gave the same warning, and took another picture.

"I'm gonna open that door."

"I'm staying here," Jill said. "No, wait, I'm coming!"

She took two steps, then aimed her flashlight left. "Look!" she said softly. "What's *that* doing in here?"

Ben had seen it too. "No idea," he said, then, "Picture," and he took a photo of a narrow iron bed along the back wall, its straw mattress rotted and falling through the slats to the floor.

"What *is* this place?" Jill whispered. "Gives me the creeps!"

Before opening the door, Ben shined his flashlight at the hinges. They were brass, blackened with age. He pushed the door gently, and the hinges squeaked a little, but they were a lot quieter than rusty iron ones would have been.

There wasn't much to see. In one corner, a wooden bucket, its rope handle nearly disintegrated. In another, a low pile of rope, and what looked like a moldy woolen coat and some scraps of leather, all thoroughly chewed by rats.

The most interesting thing to Ben's eye was immediately to his left. A low block of rusty iron sat on the floor, with the remains of a folded blanket beneath it. A good-size hammer lay nearby, and to one side of the block there was a pile of iron scraps, badly rusted. There was a scattering of clear greenish glass that might once have been a bottle. Snapping picture after picture, Ben documented everything.

"How's our time?" he asked.

"Two more minutes," Jill replied, "but I think we should leave early, don't you?"

Ben wasn't quite done. He stood in the middle of the room and did a slow turn, shooting overlapping photos. Then he went out the door, stood in the center of the area under the landing, and did the same thing. Clear pictures would help them focus their next search. And he especially wanted Robert the genius to have a good look.

"Okay," he whispered.

They both went to the low doorway and listened carefully—no sounds from nearby. Ben nodded, and Jill unlatched the hook, then pushed the panel open. Stepping out onto the stairwell floor, Jill pointed behind them. "Problem!"

They were leaving dusty footprints—and rat droppings.

Jill shut the door and pointed up at the baluster. "You do that; I'll get this," she whispered.

As Ben started up to twist the baluster closed, Jill took off the thin cotton sweater she was wearing over her T-shirt. Dropping to her knees, she swept the area clean, gathering up the rat mess in the folds of the cloth.

"Here," she said, as Ben came down. She made a face and held it out to him at arm's length. "You get to carry it."

Ben smiled. "Deal." He folded the soiled side inward until the sweater was a small blue packet, then tucked it under his arm.

They took one last look around, peeked through the hallway door, and then hurried out and walked toward the library.

They didn't meet Lyman in the hall, they got no questions or odd looks from Mrs. Sinclair as they entered the library, and there was Robert, sitting at his table, taking furious notes from a large book. He didn't even glance up at them.

Back at their place in the alcove, Ben looked at the twenty or thirty images on the tiny screen of his camera. The shots were clear, but he had no idea what he was looking at. A room, yes—but what were they supposed to find in there? And what about all that random stuff?

He shrugged. Maybe Robert would be able to make some sense of it.

Anyway, it was a successful raid. Whatever Robert's diversion was, it had worked. Ben didn't feel like they had actually found the next safeguard yet—the things they'd seen didn't seem particularly useful—yes, a few interesting antiques, but nothing like a codicil, nothing with the power to stop the Glennley Group. Still, they'd made good use of their tactical advantages. The teamwork had been perfect, and they'd proven that Lyman couldn't blockade them in the library.

The school was still theirs.

CHAPTER 10

Believable, Unbelievable

Robert munched on an onion ring, thought a moment, then said, "Simple . . . I launched a puke grenade in the south stairwell."

"A *puke* grenade?" Ben said.

Jill made a face. "I don't think I want to hear about this after all . . ."

"It wasn't *actual* puke," Robert added quickly.

"Oh . . . that's lovely," said Jill. "Because *fake* puke is ever so much more appealing. Could this maybe wait till after I finish my milkshake?"

It was almost four o'clock, and the Keepers had met up at Buckle's Diner on Central Street for a secret war council. And once they'd settled into a booth near the back, Jill had asked Robert how he had managed to keep Lyman busy after school.

"Tell me about the grenade part," Ben said.

Robert shook his head as he took a bite of cheeseburger. He enjoyed being the professor, and he wasn't about to let lowly pupils direct his lecture. He chewed slowly, took a swig of root beer, wiped his mouth, and began.

"First, with any weapon system, there's the payload, and there's the delivery mechanism—you can't really separate them. And before you begin, you have to have your objective clearly in mind. In this case, the mission was to keep Lyman away from the north staircase and, really, the whole north side of the school, for at least twenty minutes."

"But you told us we had to get out of there after *ten* minutes," said Jill.

Ben smiled to himself. Jill pretended she was all dainty, but only when she thought she *should* be. She was just as interested in this stuff as he was.

Robert held up his index finger. "Important tactical rule: Always plan for mistakes and malfunctions—it's called redundancy."

He took another bite of cheeseburger, and

kept talking as he chewed. "When you consider a weapon design, you also have to consider your enemy. In this case, we've got Lyman the Spyman—except he can't just hang around the school spying all day. To maintain his cover, he has to actually *be* the janitor. So, that's his weakness— as you already know. And really, in today's action I was sort of copying what Ben did last Friday, when he created the flood in the art room—an excellent tactical diversion that accomplished a specific objective."

Ben nodded wisely. It was nice to have his work praised by an expert.

"Okay, okay," Jill said, then paused to vacuum up the last of her shake. "Let's hear about this fake puke of yours."

A pair of elderly women in the next booth swiveled their heads and stared at Jill disapprovingly. Apparently, they did *not* want to hear about fake puke. They waved at the waitress for their check.

"Well, it's sort of like making a stew," Robert began, lowering his voice. "You have to use the right ingredients. First, I checked the school district website and found the cafeteria schedule.

Lunch at Captain Oakes today was going to be tacos, fried rice, ham and cheese on a bagel, corn, and then the regular desserts and fruit and stuff. So, to make believable vomit—"

Jill interrupted, "Most people live a whole lifetime and never get to hear the words 'believable vomit.'"

Again, the women in the next booth glared, then got up and walked to the cash register near the front door.

Robert kept talking. "I used some bits of sliced ham, some frozen corn, some lettuce, a dash of Italian salad dressing, six or seven squashed grapes, some apple juice, a chunk of chocolate cheesecake, a piece of white bread, and then the secret ingredient—milk."

"Milk?" Jill wrinkled her nose. "Why milk?"

"Ever get a sniff of that metal can in the lunchroom where you dump your trash, especially on Thursday or Friday, and especially if it's hot and humid at school? That horrible, sour, spit-uppy smell? That's spoiled milk. Anyway, late Saturday night I sealed all my ingredients into a superstrong plastic zipper bag, mooshed everything around, then put it down in the basement behind the hot-water heater—warm and dark. And nature did the rest. By Tuesday morning, I had myself a bag of first-class, weapons-grade garbage, also known as the puke grenade."

Jill made a face. "You should file for a patent."

"And your delivery system?" Ben asked.

Robert shook his head sadly. "Primitive—and dangerous. I had to deploy it by hand. I left the library, got around to the south stairwell without being seen, and ran up five flights. Then I backed down from the landing between the second and third floors, squeezing the payload out of the plastic bag. I slimed six steps plus the wall—a believable pattern."

"So . . . how did it *smell*?" Jill whispered, leaning forward. It was like she was watching a horror movie—the part that's so awful you can't look away.

"Perfect," Robert said, then added proudly, "I almost puked myself!"

Ben held up a hand, like a student in class. "But what I don't get is, why did you tell us to wait eight minutes—*exactly*?"

"Ah—this is the good part, and also the part that reveals how close I am to being truly crazy.

Because I notice things, and I always remember everything I notice. You know how I stay after school to get help and do extra work and stuff? Well, Mrs. Hinman has a daughter in day care, and Tuesday, Thursday, and Friday, she leaves school at *exactly* ten after three. So I knew when she'd be walking down the south stairwell, *and* I knew that on her way past the office she would tell Mrs. Hendon about the mess, *and* I knew Mrs. Hendon or the principal would call Lyman and order him to get it cleaned up right away before smelly stuff got tracked around. I timed all that out and calculated that by 3:18, Lyman would be busy for at least twenty minutes—*and* he'd be on the exact opposite side of the school from where you guys were."

Ben nodded, and he raised his soda glass in a toast. "Very cool—the Stealth Bomber delivers!"

"Anybody could've done it," Robert said modestly.

Jill laughed. "You don't believe that for one second, and neither do we. You're the right kid in the right place at the right time."

Ben looked at the large neon clock on the wall behind the counter. "Speaking of time, I've got to go, so here's where we are. First of all, Robert, Lyman knows we disarmed that door—which means he's probably pretty sure we've been inside again."

He explained about the note in his locker and the tape, and that Lyman had probably figured out they had Mr. Keane's keys.

Robert gave a low whistle. "This guy's not messing around."

"You've got that right," said Ben. "From now on, we should assume that he's got *some* way of checking every door, and he might try to set up cameras or listening devices too. I think he's getting desperate to know what we're doing. Oh, and *nobody* leaves anything important in any locker at any time, okay? Now, about the new room, we're going to have to get back in under those stairs again, but I'm not sure when it'll be safe. Robert, you want to think about that some more?"

"Sure thing."

"And do you have an e-mail account, some place I can send you the photos I took in there today? It ought to be an e-mail account your family doesn't use."

As they exchanged information, Jill said,

"Maybe there's a place at school where we can leave notes for Robert—no, that's silly. If we're careful, we can always talk a little in math or social studies or chorus. It's not like Lyman's got eyes everywhere."

"Okay then," said Ben. "Everybody has to study today's photos, Robert's going to think about another diversion plan, and we're all gonna be *super* careful where we leave any information. Anything else?"

They spent another few minutes counting out money for their food, and then walked outside. It was clouding up, and Ben could smell rain on the breeze from the east.

"See you tomorrow," Robert said, then walked west on Oak Street.

Jill and Ben crossed Central and walked downhill on Water Street.

Jill smiled and said, "Robert's amazing, don't you think?"

"Yeah, really," agreed Ben. "I'm glad he's on *our* side."

When they came to where Madison Street split off to the left, Jill said, "Meet you tomorrow at seven thirty, okay? Unless it's raining hard. I've got to take my cello to school for orchestra, so my mom might drive me."

"I'll be there, rain or shine. See you."

Ben walked on, thinking about Wednesday morning . . . and then remembered something— he'd meant to buy some cinnamon rolls to take home for tomorrow's breakfast. He turned around and started walking back up to Buckle's.

Glancing to his right down Madison Street, he saw Jill jogging, already half a block away. When he'd walked uphill another twenty feet or so, he reached the point where he could see the diner.

A man wearing a gray hoodie and a Patriots cap came out the door, looked both ways, then went around the corner onto Oak Street and climbed into a pickup. As the truck pulled out and turned left, Ben got a good look at the pickup and a clear view of the driver's profile.

And that's when he knew for sure—it was Lyman.

Ben spun around and hurried downhill again, his mind racing.

Had Lyman been there the whole time? But . . . *how?* He couldn't have been sitting close to them . . . *could he?*

Right away, Ben stitched together some possibilities. If Lyman had followed Jill and him when they left school, then he would have seen them meet up with Robert on Central Street and go into the diner. So then . . . Lyman could have just pulled up the hood on his sweatshirt, slouched through the door, slid into a booth near the front, and opened up a newspaper. It had to be something like that . . . very smooth.

His logical appraisal of Lyman's skills didn't keep Ben from feeling slightly sick—almost lightheaded. This was bad. And if Lyman had overheard even a *little* of what they'd talked about . . .

And the worst part? This could have been

Instantly, Ben made that thought more specific: *I could have avoided this*—and *I didn't.*

Instead of going with his first instinct and contacting Robert only by e-mail and phone, it was *his* bright idea of getting everyone together this afternoon at Buckle's. It had sounded like fun.

Fun—*bah!*

Once again, he had underestimated the enemy. And because of *his* bad leadership, Lyman had just shot down their Stealth Bomber. They'd lost an important tactical advantage, and their control of the high ground was now much less secure.

The marina came into view, and a crowd of seagulls suddenly took flight from the beach, their sharp cries cutting the air. It sounded like they were mocking him, screaming to the world, *Pratt's an idiot! Pratt's an idiot!*

Because that was exactly how he felt.

CHAPTER 11

Senior Advisers

By Wednesday afternoon, Ben was feeling less like an idiot. The chocolate cake helped a lot.

"Here, dear," Mrs. Keane said, "let me cut you another slice."

Tuesday night had been awful for Ben, a real low point.

When he'd arrived home that afternoon, he had immediately e-mailed Jill and Robert, sending them the pictures he had taken at the school, and then explaining how he'd seen Lyman coming out of the diner after their war council. He had also apologized for his lousy leadership abilities, and especially for coming up with an idea that had ruined Robert's value as their secret weapon.

Jill had replied instantly:

> Don't worry, Benjamin. Lyman still knows almost nothing. And stop kicking yourself. You're NOT the big chief, remember? You had the idea, but we ALL decided to get together today. Only 1/3 of the mess-up is your fault—democracy, remember? See you in the a.m.

Jill's reply had made him smile, but still left him feeling like they had suffered a needless defeat—a defeat that was *mostly* his fault.

However, Robert's reply had truly cheered him up:

> Pratt, chill. Okay, Lyman saw me. BUT he did *not* see *you* after you learned that he'd seen me—which means we're still in control. We just keep acting like we think L doesn't know I'm on the crew. That way, we can use *me* to feed false information to *him*—spies call it disinformation. It's a perfect setup. We're gonna have that overgrown whippet chasing his own tail and howling at the moon in no time—trust me.

Also took a quick look at the pix you took today. I've got an idea, maybe a theory. Can you send me the full text of the safeguard clues document?

What Robert said about feeding false information to Lyman had made sense to Ben. So instead of sitting around grumpy and depressed all Tuesday night, he had gotten all his schoolwork under control—because in addition to all the Keepers stuff, the math, social studies, English, and science assignments were *not* letting up. Throwing himself into homework had actually felt like a break, an escape into normality.

The three Keepers had arrived back at the battleground Wednesday morning with a plan. None of them had thought it was a good idea to try to get back under the stairs on Wednesday . . . but *everyone* had agreed to a test run of Robert's disinformation idea.

The first move happened in the cafeteria. When she was done with her lunch, Jill had passed Robert a message written on a yellow sticky note. She made the handoff secretly, but Lyman had seen it—just like he was supposed to.

Robert read the message, then tore up the note

and put all the little yellow pieces into his empty milk carton. Again, Lyman had observed. After finishing his lunch, Robert went and dumped his paper trash into the big metal barrel before he returned his tray.

Not three minutes later, Ben glimpsed Lyman carrying a large black garbage bag into the janitor's workroom—the lunchroom trash. That bag had Robert's empty milk carton in it, *plus* at least a hundred other cartons just like it.

None of the Keepers had actually seen Lyman opening up all those milk cartons until he found the right one. No one had watched him laying out all the little yellow milk-soaked bits, or reassembling those scraps into the note Jill had passed to Robert. But by the end of school on Wednesday, the Keepers *knew* that Lyman the Spyman must have done just that.

The note had been written in smudgy pencil—that was Jill's idea. If Lyman *was* able to put the torn-up note back together, he would discover that only four words were clear enough to read: "under the water fountain."

There were six gray, boxy water fountains in the original Oakes School building, two on each floor. By the time school had let out on Wednesday afternoon, Jill and Ben and Robert had spotted Lyman carefully mopping up around three different water fountains—proof that he had found Jill's note, put it back together, and then investigated the information he had read.

Of course, Lyman didn't find anything under any of the water fountains—there was nothing to find. But he must have felt like he had cleverly tapped into the secret communications of those annoying kids. He was dead wrong.

Mrs. Keane came back from the kitchen with Ben's plate, and Ben temporarily forgot about Lyman. This woman made some of the best chocolate cake ever.

They had met at her husband's funeral last week. She had thanked him for being kind to the injured janitor, and later she had given him Mr. Keane's keys. She had also asked him to stop by at her home one day after school. If he had known cake would be involved, he would have come sooner.

"Wonderful berries, Maggie, and we're not even at a funeral!"

Ben took a quick look at Mrs. Keane to see

if Tom Benton had offended her—*he* certainly would never have dared to say that to a woman whose husband had recently died.

But Mrs. Keane laughed. "Tom, I certainly hope that when *you* get to heaven, there's a big bowl of fruit waiting for you."

Tom's face wrinkled into a smile, and he raised one eyebrow. "Who says I'm going to heaven?"

Mrs. Keane laughed again. "*I* do—and probably Benjamin too, right?"

Ben's mouth was full, but he smiled and nodded. Mrs. Keane was putting on a brave front, but he'd seen her dab away a tear from the corner of her eye. All this talk about her husband wasn't easy for her. But she kept right at it.

"Now," Mrs. Keane said, "when we spoke at Roger's funeral, one of the reasons I invited you over, Benjamin, was because of his notebook—he told me to give it to you, and he said to be sure that Tom saw it too."

She showed him a small booklet with worn leather covers, not much bigger than an index card. An elastic string held it shut. The notebook was curved, and Ben knew why—when he carried note cards in his front pocket for a day or two, they took on that same shape.

Mrs. Keane pulled off the elastic and opened it up. "Most of the notes here aren't mysterious at all—hardware store lists, how to set thermostats, delivery dates, service appointments, all the hundred-and-one things a custodian has to keep track of."

She flipped through the pages, then held the book out for them to see. "But here at the back, I think this must be what he wanted you to see. There's no date on this page, but it looks like the last thing he wrote—any ideas?"

Ben and Tom leaned in close to look. There were groups of numbers with a few letters thrown in, all written in pencil. One of the number groups had been crossed out.

Ben shook his head. "Doesn't mean anything to me—how about you?"

Tom munched a grape thoughtfully. "Well . . . if I'm not mistaken, what we're looking at here . . . is a treasure map."

"A *map*?" whispered Ben. Then, "Oh, *ohhh*—I

get it! These are coordinates, right? Like on a nautical chart—latitude and longitude!"

Tom smiled and popped another grape into his mouth. "Nope. The giveaway is there in the third row. If you know what that *L* stands for, you can crack the code."

Ben's eyebrows bunched up. "Um . . . landing? Lamppost? Ladder? Locker? Lantern? Lifeboat . . ."

Then his face brightened. "Library—it stands for 'library,' right?"

"Good," said Tom. "Now, how about that number twelve?"

Ben was on his feet, pacing. "Twelve . . . that must be *room* twelve, because when you come from the office, you pass room twelve, and then comes the library!" He stopped and stared at the notebook page for a long moment. "But . . . what about the other numbers, the ones and twos?"

Tom smiled as he speared a huge chunk of pineapple with a toothpick. "First, see if you can think why *one* of the nine entries has a line drawn through it."

"Easy," Ben said. "Mr. Keane was crossing it off—like that one didn't matter anymore."

"Okay," said Tom, wiping off his chin with a lacy little napkin, "now think: On that last day when he told Maggie to give this to you, he said *I* should see it too. What was the very last thing Roger—Mr. Keane—told *me* about?"

Ben tapped his tongue against the back of his front teeth a few times—then smiled. "The tackle box, the coins! He found one batch of coins—the one he crossed off—and these? He thinks another *eight* are waiting! That's it! That *has* to be it!"

"Almost," Tom said. "By my count, there are *ten* other hiding places to find: *one* between rooms four and six, *two* between rooms seven and nine, and so on—first floor, second floor, third floor."

Tom's smile broadened. "Now, a good magician isn't supposed to explain his tricks, but I've got a confession to make here—in case you were wondering how I solved this so easily. When this business about tearing the school down heated up this spring, I told Roger how I'd solved the clue on the gold coin and located the big key and list of clues. And right away, Roger noticed something I never did—twelve other places around the school with short lengths of baseboard molding, like the one up on the third floor. And when he opened up the one on the second floor between rooms twenty-three and twenty-five, he found something, and left me that phone message about my tackle box."

"So, we should go and open up all the rest of them, right?" Ben said. "'Cause if there really *is* more gold and silver, that could add up to a *lot* of cash!"

"Well," Tom said, "would *any* amount of money make the Glennley people change their plans? I'm not sure hunting for more coins is the best use of your time right now. Finding the rest of those safeguards should probably come first . . . at least, that's how I see things."

Ben was quiet, thinking—they all were. Looking past Mrs. Keane, Ben noticed a photo in a simple wooden frame on the table beside the couch, a young couple on their wedding day. He was sure the woman was *Mrs.* Keane, but that guy, was *that* . . . ?

Mrs. Keane saw the look on Ben's face and followed his gaze.

She smiled and said, "Benjamin, I want to tell you a little story about my Roger, not the gruff old custodian, but the man I married. Now, I've never told this to another soul—and I expect you to keep this in confidence, all right?"

After Ben nodded, she continued. "When Roger got out of the navy we got married, and we were very poor. Then Tom here got Roger the job at the school. We were so happy about that. I had a job at a bakery, and we both worked long hours, trying to save enough to buy a house. Well, a year or so after we'd been married, Roger came home to our rented rooms late one Friday evening in May and told me to pack a bag, because this was finally our honeymoon weekend—we'd never had the time or the money before then. I told him he was being foolish, but I packed, and we got in the car, and then that silly man made me put on a blindfold. He drove for almost two hours. I napped most of the time, and I had no idea where we were going. He finally stopped, and we walked into a hotel . . . it must have been nearly midnight—and me still wearing the blindfold! The desk clerk said, 'Welcome, sir. I'm sorry, but our elevator's out of order until morning. May I carry those bags to your room?' And Roger said, 'Yes, we are Mr. and Mrs. Keane, and I reserved the honeymoon suite.'

"We followed the clerk up the stairs, and when we finally got to our room, Roger gave him a tip and closed the door. Then he came up behind, and took off my blindfold. And I blinked, and I found myself facing a window, looking out at the biggest, brightest moon I have ever seen. There was moonlight on the water, and a soft ocean breeze, and we were standing in room thirty-four at the Captain Oakes School. The desks were all gone, and there were lace curtains on the windows, and there was a four-poster bed and a washstand, and right down the hall there was a girls' room and a boys' room."

Smiling at Tom, she said, "All our gourmet meals were delivered to our door by that wonderful desk clerk, and we stayed at the 'Captain Oakes Hotel' until Sunday afternoon. It was the *best* seaside honeymoon any bride could ever wish for!"

She dabbed at her eyes with a napkin, then looked Ben full in the face, dead serious. "Benjamin, if there is anything, *anything* I can do to help keep our school right where it is, you ask me, all right? Will you promise me that?"

Ben looked her in the eye. "I promise. And . . . and thanks for telling me about . . ." He started to say, "your honeymoon," but that sounded too personal, so he said, ". . . all that."

"Now, more cake?" she asked. "Or another glass of milk?"

Ben's phone made two sharp vibrations in his pocket. "No, thanks," he said. "Um, excuse me, but I need to check my phone. This might be Jill or Robert."

It was Robert.

I was on School Street when I saw L drive away. I doubled back n Mrs. Sinclair let me in. Had to check out an idea—I was right.

S staircase has a room just like the N one does! Went in—and think I found the safeguard. Number 11 stamped on one side, EBTC and an eagle on the other. Ideas?? Home now—call!

The photo attached to the text showed something that looked like a dog tag next to a quarter for size comparison.

"Are you all right, dear?"

Ben looked up quickly. Tom and Mrs. Keane seemed worried—the expression on his face must have alarmed them.

"Yeah . . . yeah—it's just . . . Robert thinks he found the safeguard—some kind of metal tag!"

He held out his phone, and they both looked at the image. "Number eleven is stamped on one side, and EBTC and an eagle are on the other."

Mrs. Keane and Tom exchanged a quick look.

"What?" Ben said. "What? You know what that means?"

Mrs. Keane nodded. "Almost anybody in this town who's our age knows what EBTC means—that's the Edgeport Bank and Trust Company."

Tom added, "I've got a key to a safe-deposit box at home stamped with EBTC and an eagle, except my number is 1076. Edgeport Trust was one of the first banks outside of Boston . . . the captain must have stored something there."

Ben frowned. "But . . . if he had his own huge building for hiding things, why would he keep stuff there?"

Tom shrugged. "Only one way to find out."

CHAPTER 12

The Ones Who Showed Up

At three thirty the next afternoon a fivesome walked into the lobby of the Edgeport Bank and Trust Company—the three Keepers plus their two senior advisers. Anyone glancing at them would have guessed it was Grandma and Grandpa running an errand with three of their grandkids.

A young woman wearing a blue pantsuit came over to the group, her heels clicking on the marble floor. She had short dark hair and a friendly smile.

"Welcome to Edgeport Trust—may I help you?"

She was surprised when it was Ben who stepped forward. "Yes, please. We have a token from the bank, number eleven." He held it out for inspection, but didn't offer to hand it to her.

She leaned in closer. "Hmm . . . interesting." She ushered them past a velvet rope at the boundary of the main lobby and pointed at a waiting area with comfortable armchairs and low coffee tables. "Please take a seat while I go and make an inquiry for you."

Three minutes passed, and Ben was starting to feel like they'd been forgotten. It was so quiet he could hear a large grandfather clock ticking from twenty feet away. One of the tellers behind the high granite counter began counting money, and every bill made a crisp little hiss.

Robert wandered over to a tall brass table and began studying the deposit and withdrawal slips. He looked around a little, then took a lollipop from a bowl. When Jill frowned and shook her head at him, he went back and took another one.

After another long three minutes, a trim, white-haired gentleman wearing a dark gray suit came out of a hallway to their right. He walked straight to Ben and put out his hand. "May I examine your medallion, please? I need to establish its authenticity." Ben reluctantly gave it to him, and he disappeared down the same hallway.

Less than a minute later the man was back. Ben couldn't read the expression his face—something between relief and awe. He handed the metal tag back to Ben.

In a low, carefully restrained tone he said, "All of you, kindly follow me."

Down the hallway they went, footsteps muffled by the thick carpet. After a few turns, they were led into a walnut-paneled conference room. A large rectangular table made of the same rich wood filled most of the space. The chair seats were covered in dark green leather.

Their guide pointed and said, "Please, sit."

They took chairs along one side of the table, and after closing the door, the banker sat across from them. Ben lay the brass tag on the polished wood in front of him. The man stared at the medallion a moment, then cleared his throat.

"Ahem . . . let me introduce myself. I am Arthur Rydens, and I am the senior trust officer here at Edgeport Bank and Trust Company, a financial institution that traces its roots back to the year 1790.

One of my first duties upon joining the trust department thirty-some years ago was to take complete responsibility for trust account number eleven."

He paused long enough to look each of them in the face. "Trust number eleven was established in February of 1791, which makes it the longest-lived responsibility this bank has ever had. Through more than two hundred years, one trustee after another has each done his or her best to secure and grow the assets originally placed under our care."

The man paused again and scanned the row of faces across the table. "Are there any questions?"

Tom Benton raised a hand. "Do you . . . have any snacks handy? Maybe some fruit . . . or some cold juice?"

The man shook his head. "Sorry, no. I meant, are there any questions about what I've *said* so far?"

Robert raised a hand. "Sir, how come you haven't asked us who we are?"

The banker's eyebrows shot up. "*That* is a perceptive question, young man, and it leads me to the next portion of my explanations. Ahem . . . a trust agreement involves three parties, three main participants: the *settlor*, the *trustee*, and the *beneficiary*. In simple terms, the *settlor* is the original owner of the property that is placed in trust; the *trustee* follows the settlor's orders about how that property is to be managed; and the *beneficiary* gets the results or the benefits from whatever has been left in the trust. In this case, the bank is the trustee—"

"Right," said Robert, not bothering to raise his hand this time, "we get it—someone left something with detailed instructions, you followed the instructions, and today we showed up with tag number eleven. How come you haven't asked us *anything* about who we are, or even how we got the medallion?"

The man's eyes flashed, but he kept his voice even. "*Because* the settlor's instructions state that I am to make the full assets of the number eleven trust available to whoever shows up with *that*." And he pointed at the brass tag.

"Whoever shows up?" said Robert. "You mean *anybody*—"

The man cut him off, still pointing, "Yes, *anybody* who walked in the door with *that*." He opened the folder in front of him. "Now—"

"Excuse me," Robert said, then paused, his

head tilted to one side, "but how did you know that this tag is the *real* one, and not just some fake that I made down in my basement?"

Arthur Rydens folded his arms. "I am not at liberty to reveal that information."

"So . . . who was the settlor?" asked Robert.

The banker shook his head. "The terms of the trust do not give me permission to reveal that." He glared at Robert. "May I continue now?"

"Sure," Robert said, "except we all *know* who set up the trust. But go ahead."

"Ahem . . ." The man pulled a pair of glasses from his coat pocket and perched them on the end of his nose. "The initial trust deposit was a quantity of gold coin from various countries of origin, principally Britain and Spain. We were instructed to keep that gold for a period of ten years, and then convert it into United States dollars. We were then instructed to, and I quote, 'invest the dollars in reputable American companies engaged in or supporting the business of transporting goods and/or people.' We were also instructed to continue in this same activity *indefinitely*, reinvesting whatever profits we were able to secure, on behalf of the trust."

"Do you have a list of those companies?" Ben asked.

"Certainly." The man flipped through his folder, then slid one sheet across the table.

Ben's eyes lit up as he scanned the paper, and he started reading aloud. "Clipper ship companies, wagon builders, horse farms, carriage and sleigh makers, Bath Iron Works, three different road-building companies, Wells Fargo, Anchor Line Riverboats, the Union Pacific Railroad, American Bicycle Company, Indian Motorcycle Company, American Steamship Company, Standard Oil, Goodrich Rubber Company, General Motors, Ford Motors, six trucking companies, Pan American Airways—even airplane builders like Boeing! This is the whole history of transportation!"

"Mr. Rydens," Jill said quietly, "I'd like to know about the money, please."

The banker smiled at her. "I was starting to think no one would ever ask." He riffled through more papers. "Ahem . . . after the bank sold off the gold coin in 1801, the original investment sum was fourteen thousand, three hundred and seventy-seven dollars. We have grown that amount at an annual rate of 4.2 percent—not *better* than the U.S.

stock market average since 1871, but even four percent asset growth is not easy to maintain when limited only to transportation-related sectors, if I may say so. We're actually quite proud of that."

Mr. Rydens removed his glasses, pulled a silk kerchief from his coat pocket, polished both lenses, then balanced the spectacles back on his nose.

"Ahem . . . Now, you must also bear in mind that the bank has always subtracted an annual commission, and then there are day-to-day fluctuations in the currency markets . . . and, of course, our trusteeship has spanned difficult times such as the War of 1812, the Civil War, the Panic of 1907, the First *and* Second World Wars, the Great Depression—"

"Sir, we get it," Robert interrupted, "America's total history. How much money's in the trust right now, today?"

"Ahem . . . eighty-eight million, two hundred thirty-one thousand dollars."

Mrs. Keane gasped, then silence—two seconds . . . five seconds . . .

Ben whispered, "Eighty-eight . . . *million*?"

The banker nodded. "Yes—in that region."

"That's quite . . . a region . . . isn't it?" breathed Mrs. Keane.

"It is," the man agreed. "When it comes to growing money, there's nothing quite like *time*."

Jill stammered, "And w-we can use that—that *money*—however we *want*?"

Mr. Arthur Rydens smiled for the second time. "Another *very* perceptive question. The answer is yes . . . and no. Again, I quote from the terms in the trust document: "Whoever presents the medallion for the number eleven trust shall be given unquestioned access to whatever sums may be then available, *provided* that such funds are to be used exclusively and in good faith for the welfare, preservation, and continuing operation of the Captain Duncan Oakes School, located between Washington and Ocean Streets, in Edgeport, Massachusetts.""

"But what if . . . ," began Robert, his head tilted to one side, "what if the school had burned down or something, like, a hundred years ago—would the bank have used that money to rebuild it?"

Mr. Rydens raised one eyebrow and frowned at him. "There are certain provisions in the trust that I am not at liberty to discuss—with *anyone*."

Again Ben whispered, *"Eighty-eight million dollars!"*

Robert said, "And we're *all* in charge of that money now, all five of us?"

"That is correct," said the banker. "*You* are the ones who showed up."

CHAPTER 13

Not So Sure

It was 3:22 on Friday afternoon. Ben and Jill and Robert were in the library, and Lyman had just left the room after his second visit to be sure no one was roaming the halls. He wouldn't be back for at least five minutes, so the three Keepers risked a quick conference in the alcove—they were still keeping away from Robert during school hours so Lyman would continue to believe they were trying to conceal their collaboration.

Robert slid onto the bench next to Ben and whispered, "Have you checked this area for microphones?"

Ben nodded. "Twice."

"Good." Robert smiled. "So, you guys have any

good ideas about how to use our money? I've got *tons!*"

"First of all," said Jill crisply, "it's not *our* money—there are *rules.*"

"Yeah, yeah, Miss Scrooge, I know all that, but there's still a lot of cool stuff we could really use."

Jill sniffed. "I suppose you want a big powerboat that'll do seventy miles an hour—in case Lyman tries to steal the whole school one night and tow it out to sea."

Robert made a fake smile. "Ha. Ha. Ha. You are *so* funny . . . looking. I'll continue this discussion with the *other* three members of the finance team."

Riding home from the bank on Thursday with Mrs. Keane, Jill had told Robert he'd been pretty rude to the banker, and that had led to an argument, and there had been a chill in the air ever since. Ben wanted to change the subject, but Jill kept talking.

"You *heard* Mr. Rydens, Robert. If we use *any* money, the decision has to be *unanimous*—all five of us have to sign every release form . . . just in case you forgot *that* little detail."

"So, Robert," Ben said quickly, "you never did

tell us your theory about the north staircase room."

Robert shook his head. "I don't want to say until I look at all the artifacts in there myself."

Jill rolled her eyes, and Ben knew what she was thinking. He was getting tired of Robert's attitude too. Yes, the kid *was* amazingly smart, but still . . .

Jill jumped back in. "I don't see how we're going to get in there now—I mean, Lyman *knows* we have keys, he *knows* we know about his alarm system, so he's probably adding new security measures all the time. He'd just love to catch us doing something against the school rules—or something illegal. Then we'd be *totally* messed."

Ben agreed with what Jill was saying . . . but suddenly the edge of an idea appeared, then an entire little plan popped into his mind. In a flash he knew it could work—and he blurted out the whole idea before Robert saw it—or had time to come up with something even smarter.

"Listen," he said, "how about today, *right now*, we go to every door and we peel off all of Lyman's sensors, every single one of them! No way will he have enough spares to replace all of them, and it'll take him at least a day to get more, right? We take his whole system down! And then we wait until three a.m.—even if he patrols the place himself tonight, he'll be gone by then—and we show up, choose a door, and we're in!"

Jill looked skeptical—and Ben saw she also looked hurt, like he'd turned against her. She frowned. "Well, *I* can't sneak out at three in the morning—and, Benjamin, you're staying on your dad's boat. One tiny sound and he'll hear you, you know he will."

"So . . . ," Robert said, "Pratt comes to my house for a sleepover. We can get out of *my* house easy, no problem. I really do need to *see* that stuff."

Jill shook her head. "Too risky. It's *not* worth it." She clamped her jaw shut, which made her bottom lip stick out a little.

Ben knew that look. She'd made up her mind, and she wasn't going to change it.

Robert turned and looked at Ben, one eyebrow raised. "What do *you* say, Pratt?"

He was asking, *Are you with* me *on this . . . or with* her?—and all three of them knew it.

Ben looked at Jill, hoping to bring her back in. Because he really did think this was a workable plan . . . *and* if Robert's past successes were any indication, there might actually be something important under those stairs.

But Jill looked down at the library table, her jaw still clamped.

Ben made his choice. "I'll ask my dad about a sleepover."

Robert slapped Ben on the back. "Great! Now, there are twelve doors, including the ones in the Annex, and there are three of us, so each of us just has to—"

Jill stood up, tucking her papers into her backpack. "Divide those doors by two—count me out. See you Monday."

"Come on, Jill," said Ben, "don't be like that. . . ."

"Like *what*?" she snapped. "Cautious? Intelligent? *You're* the one who's been telling everybody not to be impatient, not to rush things. Well, you're on your own for this one . . . *Pratt*."

Jill swung her book bag onto her shoulder and walked away.

Robert didn't skip a beat. "So, then how about you pull the sensors off all the doors on the south and east sides, and I'll get the doors on the north and west. And if Lyman sees us, so what? It's not like he can shove us around, or go and report us for shutting down his private surveillance system. . . ." Then Robert noticed Ben's face. "Hey," he said, "don't worry about Jill . . . she'll be back, you *know* she will."

Ben didn't feel so sure about that—and as he and Robert left the library and split up, he wondered if he was making a mistake. He could still put the brakes on this thing . . . shut it off right now, then call Jill and apologize.

But Ben didn't want to do that. After all, he'd

sneaked out once before in the middle of the night, and it'd been fun . . . sort of. And with Robert along, it'd be even more of an adventure. Actually, it might be *better* just having the two of them for a job like this . . . and as long as they were super, super careful, what did they have to lose?

Ben was standing at the front door now, his stainless-steel ruler already in his hand. He looked both ways, pushed the door wide, and reached up, sliding the end of the ruler under the bottom edge of the sensor. It came loose and dropped to the floor. He picked it up and stuck it in his pocket.

Letting the door close, he walked quickly past the office and headed for the entrance by the bus driveway. One door was disarmed, and he needed to get to five others as quickly as possible—and also try to avoid being seen by Lyman. A plan was in motion, and the tall guy was going to get a big surprise.

Ben smiled at that thought, and then made a slight correction—*My* plan is in motion.

CHAPTER 14

History, Revised

When his dad stopped the car in front of 37 Beecham Street around seven thirty, Ben thought they must be at the wrong address. Robert lived in a small saltbox-style house—not what Ben had imagined. What with his brand-new racing sailboat last year, and the way he always wore nice clothes to school, Ben had thought Robert's family must be rich or something. As he and his dad went up the front walk, Ben saw that the house needed painting, and a couple of the boards on the front steps had wide cracks—nothing dangerous, just not shipshape.

"Hey, Ben, come on in. Hi, Mr. Pratt—this is my grandmother."

Ben's dad stepped forward and shook hands with a woman in her midsixties.

She smiled warmly and kept hold of his hand. "Nice to meet you, Mr. Pratt, and I'm so glad Benjamin's come to spend the night. It gives me a chance to thank both of you in person for the way he rescued Robert the other weekend. I hope you got my thank-you note."

"Yes, thanks," Ben's dad said. "My wife mentioned that you'd written to Ben. We're proud of him, and I'm glad to see these two doing something together other than trying to be the first one to round a buoy."

"Yes, I'm sure they'll have a good time. I'll be running some errands around ten tomorrow—shall I bring him home? I've still got your address over on Walnut Street."

"Actually," his dad said, "if you could drop him off at Parson's Marina, that'd be great. He's staying there with me this week."

"All right, that's fine. Really, it's so good to meet you."

"Thanks, you too." Turning to Ben, he said, "Have a good time, and behave yourself, all right?"

"I will, Dad. Bye."

Following Robert inside and through the living room, Ben noticed that the chairs and couch weren't fancy, and that the carpeting looked a little worn. But the wooden floors were waxed and buffed, and the whole place was spotless—*completely* shipshape. The kitchen was plain as well, but orderly and clean, *and* the smell of chocolate chip cookies was in the air.

The kitchen opened into a small sunroom that had been added to the back of the house. Robert pointed at a doorway with steps down into the backyard.

He whispered, "Check it out—it's gonna be a snap to do you-know-what at you-know-when." Pointing again, he said, "Toss your sleeping bag on the couch—I'm using the cot over there. Gram said we could sleep down here in the TV room, after I begged for about twenty minutes. Pretty sweet, huh?"

"Yeah—she seems really nice," Ben said. "Are your parents out of town or something?"

"No," Robert said slowly, "they're in town, sort of. They're just . . . not alive. They're in the cemetery behind the Congregational Church. They both died in a car crash about six years ago. And my grandfather died three years ago—so here at 37 Beecham Street, it's the widow and orphan show, seven days a week. Welcome to this Friday night performance."

Ben jerked his head around to look at Robert's face—was he joking? No, couldn't be, not about that . . . and he wasn't smiling. Ben didn't know how to react, when suddenly he pulled in a sharp breath—he hadn't realized that he'd stopped breathing when Robert said that, about the car crash.

"I'm—I didn't know any of that—about—all that."

Robert shrugged. "No sweat—not many kids do. I mean, that was when I was in kindergarten, so it's not like it got talked about at school or anything. The teachers all know 'cause Gram's always at my conferences and stuff. But everything's working out okay."

Ben smiled faintly, but he didn't know what to say.

"So," Robert went on, "you want food or anything? Gram made some killer chocolate-chocolate chip cookies, and there's ice cream—all kinds of good stuff."

Ben shook his head. "No thanks—maybe later. I just ate at the steak house with my dad. Oh—I mean—yeah, I—I just ate."

Talking about his *dad*? After what Robert had just said? So *stupid*!

Ben felt his face turning red.

Robert looked at him hard. "Listen, Pratt, I get it, okay? Almost everybody else has parents, and I *don't*. It's just the way it is, and I'm okay with it. So don't get all weirded out. Sheesh!"

"Sorry," Ben said, still blushing.

"And *don't* say you're sorry, either, Pratt. I'm still the same pushy jerk I've always been, right? So lighten up . . . before I have to come over there and punch you."

Ben laughed. "Right. A jerk. And pushy . . . so true."

Robert pointed at the table by the couch. "Toss me the remote. Gram said we could watch anything as long as it's PG or PG-13 . . . wanna check out the cable listings? Or we could hook up my PlayStation. . . ."

By eleven forty-five the TV was off, but it was still warm.

Robert said, "I know it's kind of early, but if we're quiet now, Gram'll be snoring in ten minutes. Maybe we should catch some sleep too, set our phones to buzz at two thirty. What do you think?"

Ben was surprised Robert was asking his opinion. All night long he'd been the total chief about everything—the movie they'd watched ("Nah, that one stinks . . . *this* is the one we want."), their Need for Speed marathon ("I am *invincible*!"), even about the snacks ("Sour cream and onion chips are the *best*!").

Ben nodded. "Yeah, some sleep would be good."

They both set alarms, and then Robert turned off the lamp on the table by his cot. With the light out, the wide glass walls and skylights of the sunroom stopped acting like mirrors and became windows again.

As his eyes adjusted to the darkness, Ben felt like they were sleeping outside. There was no moon—he had checked the moon-phase calendar earlier. But the streetlights threw enough glow to reveal the oak and maple trees overhead, their swaying limbs outlined against the cloudy sky.

After five minutes or so, Ben could tell Robert was still awake too. It seemed kind of weird to just lie there, both of them wide awake, without saying anything. But then again, it was a welcome break. Robert had talked nonstop all night.

And anyway, what was there to talk about?

I could always tell him that he's started being pretty obnoxious again, especially to Jill. . . .

He smiled to himself at that, but instantly heard his mom's voice in his mind: *If you can't say something nice, don't say anything.*

Something nice? About Gerritt? How about *halfway* nice?

"You know tonight?" Ben said quietly. "When you said you were the same pushy jerk? That's pretty much how I always saw you."

Hmm . . . was that nice at *all*?

But Ben heard a smile in the voice that answered.

"That's not exactly a news flash, y'know." Robert paused. "So . . . what about now?"

Ben had an answer ready, and almost cracked himself up. "Progress—from a D-minus up to a C-plus."

Robert laughed softly. "Nice report card . . ." He was quiet a moment. "You know, I kind of envied how your mom and dad never missed anything you did at school—choir concerts, that art show in fourth grade, even that dumb play we did for Colonial Day . . . you were Governor Winthrop."

"And *you* got to be Captain Oakes—I was so jealous!" Then Ben added, "And I—I was also jealous of how rich you were—new clothes all the time, and when you got your boat last year? That about killed me."

"Me? *Rich?*" Robert was genuinely surprised. "You got *that* wrong, completely. When my mom and dad died, they both had insurance, and the money went into a trust fund. Gram gets paid for my expenses once a month, and she's crazy about making sure I dress nice for school. And the boat, that was a present from my uncle Mike. He's not really rich, but he doesn't have any kids, so I'm his go-to guy when he feels sad that his little brother died. I mean, it's not like I wasn't glad to get the boat and everything—but it's not the same as yours."

Ben sat up on the couch. "*Who told you about my boat?* I was gonna keep it a secret until I *crushed* you out on the bay next weekend!"

"Shhh! You're gonna wake Gram."

Ben whispered again, "Who *told* you?"

"Jill—she said your mom and dad pitched in for it . . . but you can forget about trophies, Pratt. The *sailor* wins the races, not the boat."

"Yeah, big talk."

"Big winner, you mean!" said Robert.

"Big *jerk*, is more like it" said Ben. "And pushy, too—*D-minus!*"

They both laughed a little, and then the room settled into a comfortable silence.

Ben yawned, and ten seconds later, Robert did too.

"So," Robert said, "at oh-two-thirty hours, we roll."

"You mean, at *five bells*, we roll."

"Whatever. Get some sleep, Pratt."

"Yeah, you too."

But Ben lay awake. He could hear Robert's grandmother snoring from upstairs, as predicted. A low branch scraped on the roof now and then. And in just a few minutes, he heard Robert's breathing slide into a deep, regular rhythm—waves on a beach.

He was glad Robert had explained about his parents, and about the clothes. His boat, too. That stuff really *was* a news flash. But really, it was more like learning history. You go along, and you think the world is one way, then you pick up just a few more facts, and everything changes.

Ben was pretty sure he'd never look at Robert the same way again. And he felt like that was a good thing.

He also felt like this was going to change the way he looked at the problems his own family was having.

And that was a good thing too.

CHAPTER 15

Red-Handed

Getting out of Robert's house had been as simple as waking up, pulling on black sweatshirts, grabbing their backpacks, and tiptoeing right down the steps from the sunroom.

There were no traffic sounds—not on Central Street, not even on Salem Street. Ben could tell it was low tide by the smell of the onshore breeze— sort of a rich, muddy taste in the air.

"This way," Robert said, and Ben followed. Behind his house an alleyway cut through to Oak Street.

Instead of taking Robert's normal route to school, they crossed Central onto Church Street, which took them past the Congregational Church.

Ben wondered about Robert's parents buried there in the graveyard. What was it like for him, to know his mom and dad were right there . . . and did he remember them clearly, from back when he was so little? Ben pushed all that out of his head and concentrated on staying in the shadows.

Four minutes later they were in the trees on the school grounds, coming at the building from the south. Robert whispered, "Let's take this really slow, check the place out before we try to get in. You have an idea which door we should use?"

Ben had thought about that. "I think the northeast door is still the best."

"No way," Robert said. "Lyman *knows* you've used that door. If he had any spare sensors, he'd rearm that one for sure. That's only logical."

"Yeah," Ben said, "but it's also logical that he's guessed I'm thinking like that, so he won't bother arming that door. He'd put any spare sensors somewhere else."

"Yeah . . . ," Robert said slowly, "but if he thinks you can figure that out, then he's just as likely to put one there anyway."

"Exactly," Ben said, "which means it's still

pretty much a fifty-fifty chance. But I know which key works in that door, *and* it's the entrance closest to the north staircase. So it's still the best choice."

They worked their way around to the north side of the school. There was no one on the harbor path at five minutes before three in the morning, so they ran across the last twenty yards of open ground, opened the door, and ducked inside. Ben went in after Robert and held the door open two seconds, just long enough to use his light and check for a sensor on the jamb . . . all clear.

As planned, once inside the door, they stood there in the red glow of the exit sign for a full three minutes, ready to blast back outside and take off in different directions at any hint of danger.

Ben strained, listening for even the suggestion of a threat. Nothing—only the muffled sound of waves against the seawall.

"Let's go," Robert whispered.

Ben nodded and followed him down the hallway, then left toward the north stairwell. Ben hadn't gone fifteen steps when the phone in his pocket made two sharp vibrations, an incoming text. He jerked to a stop, and so did Robert—he'd heard it too.

"Is it Lyman?" he whispered. It was the first time Ben had ever seen Robert look really scared.

Ben took a hurried look at the screen, then breathed out slowly. "It's okay—wait here." He went back to the door and opened it for Jill.

"I didn't think you were coming!" he whispered, then immediately felt like he'd put too much emotion in his voice.

Jill smiled slightly. "I've been watching for the junior burglar brigade since two thirty."

As they walked, he asked, "How'd you get out?"

"The door in our kitchen opens into the back stairs, and there's a door to the alley from the basement utilities room. Pretty simple. Then it was just keeping clear of cop cars and homeless people."

When Robert saw Jill, he grinned. "Hey, glad you came . . . and I'm sorry I was a jerk earlier, but—"

"I know, I know," said Jill, "you really, really, *really* want to see that space again. So let's get to it."

Two minutes later they were under the north stairwell stairs, and Robert was walking around with his flashlight, moving from item to item, glancing at a small notebook he'd pulled from his back pocket. "Listen," he said, writing something with his pencil, "don't touch *anything*, okay? The integrity of the site is really important."

Ben was fine with standing by the doorway, and Jill was more than happy to stay close to the exit. There was the same smell of rats, and there were fresh droppings underfoot. Shining his light, Ben saw that the spiders had been busy too, but there were far fewer cobwebs than the first time he and Jill had walked through.

When Robert went into the small adjoining room, he called out in an excited whisper, "Hey— you gotta see this!"

They went in, and Robert was crouched down beside the pile of iron scraps Ben had spotted during their first visit. "See?" he said, moving a piece of iron with the tip of his pen. "See how this piece looks pinched here, and sharp along the edge? It was cut using that hammer and some kind of iron or steel chisel. These all came off of

slaves!" Pointing, he said, "That's an ankle shackle, and these were like handcuffs. I'm sure of it. That iron bed in the next room? I looked on the Internet, and beds like that weren't made until about 1820. And those tally marks by the door? Those stand for *people*! Pretty amazing, huh? This was a hideout, part of the Underground Railroad! I'm *sure* about this!"

"Sixty-seven," Jill whispered. "That's how many

marks are by the door! This is . . . this is . . . *historic!*"

"And it would have been the perfect cover," said Ben, "a *school!* No one would have ever guessed! And right by the water? A runaway slave could just drop into a rowboat, and be on a ship for Canada in no time."

"You know what this *means*, don't you?" said Robert, his eyes bright and wide. "This means the school *stays*—instant national landmark, guaranteed! No kidding, this is *huge!* Here, Ben, get some close-up pictures of these." He pulled a wooden ruler from his backpack. "And get this in the pictures to show the scale, okay?"

Ben took out his camera and snapped half a dozen shots.

"And get the iron block, too," Robert said. "That was the—"

"*Shhh!*" Jill hissed, holding up her hand. *"Did you hear that?"*

Everyone stopped breathing.

And then everyone heard a door slam . . . and then the sound of footsteps . . . heavy steps with half a second between each one . . . the kind of footsteps a grown man would take . . . a *tall* man.

Jill and Ben had the same exact thought. Both of them dashed back to the heavy triangular door—they'd left it standing open a couple of feet. Jill pulled the door shut gently, and Ben latched the iron hook. Robert stood frozen in the middle of the space below the landing, his face the same color it had been when Ben pulled him to safety two weeks ago. "This is *nuts*!" he whispered. "Janitors don't come to school at three in the morning!"

"No," Ben hissed, "but industrial spies *do*! Lights off!"

They heard the heavy footsteps on the wooden floor. Ben could tell that Lyman wasn't hurrying. He was working his way along the first-floor hallway. Trying to estimate the man's location was hard, but it sounded like he might be walking in the front hall, going past the office . . . yes. And now past room 12, headed for the library. The footsteps stopped every so often . . . right—Lyman was turning doorknobs, probably shining a flashlight into every room, making sure things were locked up tight.

Ben realized that this was proof that Lyman did *not* have an alarm system in place. He was

doing old-fashioned surveillance, low-tech, boots-on-the-ground legwork. Which meant that he wasn't searching for them, he was just making his rounds, like a cop walking around the block.

He began to breathe easier.

But another sound made him jump like he'd been stuck with a pin.

"Woof . . . woof."

A dog . . . a big one!

Jill must have jumped too—she bumped Ben in the dark, then grabbed hold of his hand.

They all heard the dog's feet now, keeping pace with Lyman, its long toenails clicking on the wooden floor, and both sounds came closer and closer.

Then the door into the stairwell opened, and the dog was inches away—Ben could hear it sniffing. And then Lyman's deep voice.

"What've you got there, Moose?"

That little bit of encouragement got the dog excited, and he barked two huge *woof*s. Jill clamped Ben's hand so tightly his fingers tingled.

The dog went quiet again, just sniffing . . . and Ben heard another sound, just behind him down near the floor, a little scritching sound—a rat!

The dog went crazy, barking and growling and pawing at the paneling like a thing possessed.

"Moose—come!" Lyman growled. "It's just a rat . . . wouldn't even taste good."

Lyman's footsteps sounded on the stairs above their heads, clomped across the landing and up the next flight.

The dog whined and scratched at the wood again.

"Moose—*come*!"

Moose's nose knew there was more than a rat behind that woodwork, but he obeyed, his toenails clicking as he scrambled up the stairs to his master.

The door wheezed open, and they listened to Lyman's heavy boots as he made a complete circuit of the second-floor hallway. Then a distant door banged shut, followed by more regular footsteps as he went up to the third floor and repeated his rounds.

Ben was amazed how the wooden timbers of the old building carried sound. It was like being inside a big drum. Lyman's distant footsteps began tapping out a regular rhythm . . . must be coming down the south stairs. Ben tried to count the footsteps—more than fifty. So he had to be on the first floor again.

It was quiet for several minutes, and Ben thought he must have left . . . then a loud metallic *clang* echoed through the building.

After that, complete silence. Jill still had hold of his hand. They all stood in the dark for several more minutes.

Robert whispered, "I think he's gone, don't you?" He clicked on his flashlight just as Jill dropped Ben's hand.

"That was a close one," she said. "I thought Moose was going to have an early breakfast—us!"

Ben smiled at her. "Nice work not freaking out when that rat started scratching around."

"It wasn't a rat," she said, grinning. "*I* made that sound with my shoe, down near the floor—I wanted Lyman to hear it and call off the dog."

"Brilliant!" said Robert. "A rat for a rat!"

Ben said, "Nice! But listen, can we get out of here now? Gerritt, do you have enough proof?"

The answer to that was no, and he had Ben take another ten or twelve pictures, especially of the heavy anvil block and the hammer.

"That should do it," Robert said. "I figure we show the pictures to Jill's mom and maybe that guy who was here taking the tools away last weekend, get the Historical Society to line up someone from a preservation group. Then we bring them to the school, show them the hideout, and *zap!*—game over."

Ben unlatched the door and swung it open. Jill stepped out first, then Robert. As Ben came out and then pushed the panel shut, he noticed Robert was standing at the fire door, still as a statue.

"Um, guys," he whispered, "we better . . . um . . ." His voice trailed off into a soft hum.

"What?" said Ben.

Robert pointed through the window, and Ben came to look.

A huge Rottweiler snarled and launched himself at the wire-reinforced glass of the door, his teeth snapping shut inches from Ben's nose. The door rattled from the force of the impact, and Ben jumped away, knocking Robert backward so he stumbled into the steps. Moose snarled and threw his weight at the door again.

Ben's heart began pumping so fast he had trouble catching his breath, but his mind snapped clear as a cold front, icy sharp.

This was bad. The dog had the three of them bottled up in the stairwell. They could go up to the second floor and go down the south stairs, but they'd have the same problem over there—Moose could probably run to that door in about fifteen seconds, not nearly enough time to safely reach an exit.

Lyman wasn't in the building now—that was clear. Otherwise, he'd have already come to check out the commotion. So . . . Lyman had left his dog in the school . . . which meant he'd be coming back for him fairly soon—maybe any moment.

Ben turned to Robert and Jill. The exit sign spread a reddish glow over their faces. "Any ideas?"

Robert shook his head. Even in the warm light, his face looked cold and ashy. He gulped. "I'm just . . . really scared of dogs."

Jill didn't seem scared, more annoyed that it was happening at all. "It's pretty clear. We've got to switch places. If we can get the dog in the stairwell, *we* can get to an exit."

Moose was on his hind legs

now, nose against the glass, whining and snarling nonstop. Ben found it difficult to think.

Jill looked at the door, then up at the stairs, then back at the door. "I think I happen to have the right secret weapon with me," she said.

Robert perked up a little. "A tranquilizer dart?" he said. "That might work."

Jill shook her head and smiled a little. "Nope." She reached deep into the pocket of her hooded sweatshirt and pulled out a small white rectangle. "Dental floss."

Robert looked at her. "Why do you have—?"

Jill cut him off. "It's a long story. Ben, you and Robert go up to the second floor, around to the south stairwell, and down to the first floor. We've got to get the timing right, so when you get there, send me a text. When I text back that I'm ready, open the ground-floor door an inch or so, and yell for Moose."

The dog at the window heard his name and tipped his head sideways a moment, glaring into the stairwell. Then he growled and snarled and snapped again.

Jill went on, "The dog hears you call, and runs over there."

Ben saw her plan. "I get it," he said.

By this time Robert got the idea too. "Here." He pulled his wooden ruler out of his pack. "This ought to help." Then he said to Ben, "Let's go."

In less than two minutes Ben texted one word: Here!

Jill stepped to the left of the door, back against the wall. She stood still for almost a minute to let the dog calm down a little. Then she texted one word back to Ben: Go!

Two voices echoed through the hallways. "Here Moose, here Moosie boy! Come here, Moose, come on, boy!"

The dog was gone like a shot, his toenails skittering, trying to get traction on the waxed wood like a kid wearing dull hockey skates.

Jill pushed her door open cautiously, just an inch, double-checking. Moose was gone, barking in full voice at the other stairwell.

She pushed the door outward one foot and propped it open with the ruler, sliding it up as high as she could reach. Jill had broken off a short length of the floss, six feet or so. It was tied to the ruler, and she looped the other end around the outer doorknob. The end coming from the dental floss container was also tied tightly to the ruler, and Jill hurried up the steps backward, pulling the thin fiber off the spool like a fisherman paying out line. She got to the landing, and then backed up the next ten steps. She opened the door and went into the second-floor hallway, then let the door close, keeping it open just a crack with her foot. She made a few turns of the dental floss around her hand, gently taking up all the slack in the line.

With one hand she texted again: Stop.

The yelling at the south stairwell stopped, and it was her turn.

"Moose! Hey, Moosie Moosie Moose! Come and get me, Moose. Here I am, boy, come on! Hey, Moosie Moosie Moose!"

She heard the dog running back her way, heard it take a spill when it took the turn by the library too fast, heard its toenails scrabbling closer, and then the dog was through the door and into the stairwell and up the first flight, leaping three steps at a time, low growls heaving from his chest.

Jill yanked on the floss and heard the ruler hit the floor, and then the lower door clanked shut. She shoved her door closed just as Moose threw his weight against it.

"Good boy, Moose, good boy," she said through the door, and got snarls in reply. She felt sorry for the dog. Her aunt Sarah up in New Hampshire had a Rottweiler, and it was a big, lovable sweetheart. "Poor fella," she said out loud. "It's all right—your master'll be back soon, I just bet he will."

And that thought set her off at a trot for the south stairwell.

By the time she got into the first-floor hallway, the other two were already back over at the north stairwell—on the outside of the door.

As Jill came running up, Robert had just taken the loop of floss off the doorknob. He knelt down in front of the door and gently pulled the string while Ben banged on the glass to keep Moose occupied. Robert eased his ruler under the door, and then yanked all the rest of the dental floss out as well.

They didn't even pause for high fives. The three of them ran toward the art room, then down the causeway and right out the doorway on the south side. They streaked past the lighted area near Captain Oakes's gravestone and didn't stop until they were out in the deep darkness beneath the largest tree on the school grounds, a giant copper beech that was over a hundred and fifty years old.

"Whew!" Ben said, totally winded. "*That* was amazing!"

Jill took a minute to catch her breath. Then she said, "Robert, I have to apologize. You were right about this. That little room is definitely the most important thing we've found yet. It's a total game changer, and you *nailed* it."

Robert sounded almost modest when he answered. "Well, if you hadn't showed up tonight, Pratt and I would still be dog food—or maybe in a police van by now."

Ben said, "Listen, we've gotta get out of here before Lyman comes back. How about we walk home along the harbor?"

Jill shook her head. "I'm fine getting back by myself—nobody'll even see me."

"I just think we all need to look out for each other," Ben said, "and this way no one has to walk home alone."

Jill said, "It's okay with me. Let's go."

If it hadn't been so dark, Ben might have noticed the slightest hint of a blush on Jill's cheek.

And in stronger light, Jill would have noticed Ben's smile for sure.

CHAPTER 16

Connected

Robert's grandmother dropped Ben off at Parson's Marina around ten fifteen on Saturday morning. He stumbled along the pier out to the *Tempus Fugit*, opened the hatch, and walked down through the galley, through the saloon, and into his forward cabin. He dropped his backpack on the deck, then dropped himself like a rock onto his bunk.

His dad came to the doorway. "Hey, Ben— you have a good time at Robert's last night?"

Ben lifted his head an inch or so. "What? Oh . . . oh, yeah. A good time. Stayed up really late . . ." His head hit the pillow again.

His dad smiled and closed the cabin door.

• • •

Around twelve fifteen Ben started swatting at a fly. It buzzed around and around his head. He knocked it away, but a few minutes later it was back, buzzing again.

Then he realized it wasn't a fly.

He sat up on his bunk, frowning at the sour taste in his mouth. He reached for his phone as it vibrated for the third time. It was a text from Jill to him and to Robert—three words: Chk yr email.

Ben moved to his desk, sat down stiffly, and fired up his laptop.

There was an e-mail from his mom—two days old. And then there was an ad for new sailing gear, a random assortment of spam, and there was something from . . . the Glennley Group?

What . . . ?

Ben clicked, and the document opened up.

The e-mail had been sent to Jill's mom at her Historical Society address, and then Jill had forwarded it to him and Robert.

It was a press release.

The Glennley Group • Arlington, VA
-----------For Immediate Release-----------

TALL SHIPS AHOY! TO INCLUDE UNDERGROUND RAILROAD EXHIBIT

As our newest theme park—Tall Ships Ahoy!—prepares for its grand opening next June in Edgeport, Massachusetts, we are pleased and proud to announce an important and historic discovery.

Under a staircase in the Duncan Oakes School, a transfer station of the Underground Railroad has recently been found, including many artifacts from the pre–Civil War era. There is no doubt of the authenticity of this discovery.

Just today the Glennley Group has reached an understanding with representatives of the African American Heritage Preservation Foundation, the National Park Service, and the National Register of Historic Places. We have pledged to preserve *intact* a significant portion of the old school building, and to reverently include this structure as a separate exhibit within the framework of our historical theme park.

The Oakes School Underground Railroad Station will be open to all Americans and to visitors from around the globe, free of charge. It is our hope that more than fifty thousand visitors each year will have the opportunity to see firsthand this dramatic and sobering window into our nation's past, and to ponder with us the historic quest of African Americans for their God-given freedom and dignity.

Contact: H.Robinson.Carling@GlennleyGroup.com

Ben read the release once, then a second time, trying to process what it meant. Halfway through the third reading, it hit him: *No one turned the baluster! We left that triangular door unlocked!*

And that giant dog had been stuck in the stairwell, sniffing and clawing away at that woodwork. When Lyman came and found the dog in the stairwell, he must have discovered the hideout . . . and then the whole Glennley organization kicked into high gear. It seemed incredible that they'd been able to act so quickly, but a company that was paying a man like Lyman to stay on-site and protect its interests had probably developed plans for all the possible things that might keep Tall Ships Ahoy! from moving forward—including another push to landmark the building.

Ben was angry, crushed, completely deflated— and it didn't help that he felt exhausted.

Last night had been such a high point, a huge victory. And now . . .

He clenched his fists and shut his eyes tight to hold back tears. He almost sobbed.

His phone buzzed again—another text. Robert this time:

Saw that thing from GG—bummer, huh? No biggie. It's just a bunch of words. There's still time, and a codicil, and a ton of cash. More safeguards too. Later—WOOF!

Ben smiled, but then shook his head. For a kid so smart, Robert could still act like he was an idiot. And if he didn't see that this was a *massive* loss, then he was either truly stupid, or just kidding himself.

Jill didn't text. She called.

Ben couldn't face some kind of phony pep talk, so he pressed the reject button and sent her to voice mail. A minute later his cell phone made a ding—she'd left a message.

Ben stood up from his desk and lay down on his bunk, staring up at gray sky through a porthole. He selected Jill's message and pushed PLAY.

"Hi, Ben. I'm looking in my crystal ball, and I see you. Stop feeling so sad about this, okay? It's amazing we didn't all end up at the police station last night. And not locking that space? It just happened, that's all. We all forgot about it. And Moose? He was just doing his thing—you can't ask a dog not to be dog, right? And that goes for Lyman, too.

It's actually pretty impressive, how fast Glennley moved on this, don't you think? Anyway, call me. Okay?"

Ben took a deep breath and pushed it out slowly. Then he scrolled to Jill's number and punched CALL. Might as well get it over with—she'd just ring him again and again till he answered.

"Hi," she said. "I left you a message."

"Yeah, I got it. Thanks."

"Did you hear from Robert?"

"Yup," he said, "how about you?"

"Just a text. Said he wasn't worried about it. Do you believe him?"

"Yeah . . . but I don't know if it's intelligence or stupidity that keeps him happy. It could also be that he just doesn't care about this like I do."

"Look," Jill said, "I know you're really serious about this, but you can't let it get to you. And besides, last night wasn't a total loss."

"Yeah?" Ben said. "How do you figure?"

"Well, we're trying to keep the school from being torn down, right? And now we know that the northwest corner of the place is going to stay right where it is, forever. So that's *something*, isn't it?"

"I guess so."

Jill was quiet a moment. "And there was something else good about last night."

"What?" he asked.

"I got to hold your hand in a dark room for five whole minutes . . . of course, I *was* terrified of being chewed to bits and then arrested, but still. Five whole minutes."

Ben smiled, then laughed a little—just enough to let Jill know that he liked what she'd said.

"I'm glad you counted that in the 'good' column," he said. Then he added, "But . . . if *Robert* had been the one there next to you, don't you think you'd have held *his* hand?"

"Maybe," she said. "But it wouldn't have been the same."

Ben smiled again, but this smile he kept for himself. Just like that, he felt as if Jill had rescued him from drowning.

Jill knew he was fine now too.

"So," she said "I'll see you Monday—if not sooner. Okay?"

"Yup. See you Monday. If not sooner. And thanks for calling, Jill."

"Thanks for calling back, Benjamin. Bye."

Ben put the phone down and closed his eyes,

lacing his fingers together behind his neck.

The sailboat rocked gently in its berth, and Ben had this feeling of being connected, but also floating free. If they pushed off from the pier, the *Tempus Fugit* could sail anywhere—the water of Barclay Bay was connected to all the other water on the planet. It was all one big thing.

Would the Captain Oakes School still be there on the shore at the end of June? Ben felt completely sure that even if the Keepers lost this war—even if the school was destroyed and the town was changed—it wouldn't be the end of the world.

Yes, he did think one way would be better, and he wasn't backing down from that, not for a second.

But all *he* could really do was his best, each moment. That was what mattered most—even more than the final outcome. Because the final outcome wasn't up to him alone.

The history of the school was one thing. The history of Benjamin Pratt was something else.

At that moment, Ben wasn't mad at Lyman, or his dog. He wasn't mad at the Glennley lawyers, or any of the people in town who wanted to tear down the school. And he wasn't mad at his mom or his dad about the way their family was right now.

Ben opened his eyes. The view through the porthole above him had improved. There were patches of blue, with clouds scudding from south to north.

It might be a decent afternoon for sailing.

KEEP
A LOOKOUT
FOR BOOK 4 IN THE
BENJAMIN PRATT & THE
KEEPERS OF THE SCHOOL
SERIES

Also by Andrew Clements